THE INNER EYE

*edited by Nicholas Humphrey
and Robert Jay Lifton*

IN A DARK TIME

The Inner Eye

NICHOLAS HUMPHREY

with illustrations by Mel Calman

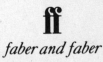

faber and faber

LONDON · BOSTON

in association with
Channel 4 Television Company Ltd

First published in 1986 by
Faber and Faber Limited
3 Queen Square London WC1N 3AU

Photoset and printed in Great Britain by
Redwood Burn Ltd, Trowbridge, Wiltshire

British Library Cataloguing in Publication Data

Humphrey, Nicholas
 The inner eye.
 1. Consciousness.
 I. Title
 153   BF311
 ISBN 0–571–13824–1

for Pamela Lindars

Contents

Introduction

Last year I returned with a television crew to the place where, fourteen years ago, I spent three of the most important months of my life. It was while watching the mountain gorillas of Rwanda that I first became interested in a philosophical and scientific puzzle which has fascinated me ever since: the problem of how a man or animal can know what it is like to be itself. This book, and the television programmes that accompany it, describe where those original speculations led.

When I went to Africa in 1971, I had been working for some years as an experimental psychologist, first in the Psychological Laboratory at Cambridge, then in the Institute of Psychology at Oxford. I had never doubted – and still do not – that psychology, the scientific study of the mind, ought to be the most exciting and challenging branch of all the sciences. But I was less and less convinced that the work I was doing then, on the brain mechanisms which underlie behaviour, was going to yield satisfying answers to the nature and origin of higher mental processes. Like so many other would-be students of the mind, I had gone to sea to see the world, only to discover that all I was seeing was sea. Not even that: I was down below decks, studying the engine room of mental life, with no clear sense of where the ship was steering.

I returned to Cambridge in 1970, this time to the Sub-Department of Animal Behaviour at Madingley. There I came into close contact for the first time with scientists of a new kind, whose roots lay not in experimental psychology but in zoology and natural history. Ethologists study behaviour first of all in a state of nature, in the wild; and they see the mind and the brain not simply as pieces of complex machinery which just happen to exist, but as organs of survival, adapted through a long history of natural selection to meet the particular needs of the particular animal in its environment. Madingley gave me a new way of looking at human and animal behaviour. It was from there that I went to study the gorillas; and it was under the influence of the ethological approach I learned from William Thorpe, Robert Hinde and Patrick Bateson that I developed the ideas that have gone into this book.

Two years ago I was engaged by Channel Four to make a series of television programmes about the evolution of human consciousness and psychological insight. We realized at once that we had something of a problem. Television viewers, I was assured, expect to be told *the truth* in 'science programmes'. When I protested that in several areas I was not at all sure what the truth was, worse still that I was not sure that it mattered what the truth was so long as one way of looking at things made 'better sense' than another, it left everybody confused. We decided, therefore, to devote a whole programme to discussing the nature of truth and 'making sense' – and, for reasons which I hope will become apparent, we decided to do it in Tahiti.

That is where the book begins. I go on to discuss

the evolution of intelligence and its relation to social life, and so to a theory about the development and uses of human consciousness. Consciousness, it has been argued, may serve a hundred purposes – or none. But in evolutionary terms I suspect that the possession of an 'inner eye' served one purpose before all: to allow our own ancestors to raise social life to a new level. The first use of human consciousness was – and is – to enable each human being to understand what it *feels* like to be human and so to make sense of himself and other people *from the inside*. There is, however, no guarantee that human beings will use this gift of insight: the last section of the book looks at some of the consequences of denying or forgetting that no one else is less human than ourselves.

The book was written during the last months of the making of the series, while the ideas and the discussions I had with the directors of the programmes were still fresh in my mind. It is not strictly a book of the series, but covers much of the same ground. Making television is difficult. I owe a huge debt to Robert Bee and Christopher Sykes, and the executive producer, Andrew Snell, each of whom has been a source of inspiration. Jane Chrzernowska, David Boardman and Simona Segre have been imaginative researchers. Carol Haslam at Channel Four oversaw the project from the start. To all of them, my thanks.

Mel Calman has done the drawings. He was, I should say, given an unusual brief: not to illustrate the book but to respond to it. Calman's little man who pops up in these pages has an independent voice, and it has been my pleasure – as I hope it will be yours – to have him commenting on and adding to the text.

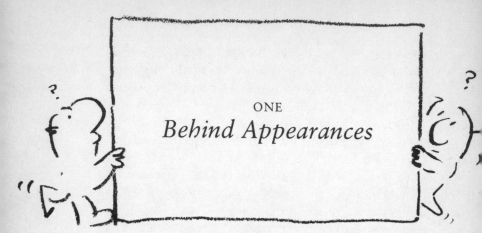

ONE

Behind Appearances

Tahiti may seem a strange place to begin. It is a tiny volcanic island in the middle of the South Pacific ocean, about as far away from anywhere as you can get. But Tahiti has an historical significance quite out of proportion to its size and place. The first explorers arrived there at the end of the eighteenth century. They took back to Europe their tales of the island and its enigmatic people. And this same island became a sort of philosophical Atlantis. Philosophers philosophized about it. Sailors in the dockyards gossiped about it. Novelists romanced about it. Painters painted it.

Captain Cook, Herman Melville, Robert Louis Stevenson, Rupert Brooke, Paul Gauguin and Charles Darwin all came to the island with different hopes and expectations. For all of them, Tahiti seems to have been a kind of natural laboratory for the imagination. It made them wonder: and because the place itself could not produce the answers to their questions, they had to find those answers from within themselves.

Gauguin first arrived there in 1891. 'I wish to live in peace', he said in an interview for a French newspaper before he sailed from Europe, 'and to avoid being influenced by our civilization. I only desire to create a simple art ... to steep myself in virgin nature, to see no one but savages, to share their life and to have as my sole occupation to render, just as a child would do, the images of my own brain.'[1]

But would these images bear much relation to what he encountered on the surface? Not always. Shortly after coming to Tahiti he wrote an account of his life among the savages: *Noa-Noa*, Fragrance-Fragrance – a book which, to anyone who has actually visited Tahiti, does indeed have a strange smell.

Along the coast from Gauguin's village is a water-filled cave, the Grotte de Maraa, where Gauguin went swimming with his native wife, Tehura.

'Will you come with me?' I asked Tehura, pointing to the end. 'Are you mad? It's very far ... and the eels. No one ever goes there!' ... But I set off, my heart beating at the prospect of going alone. I experienced the strange illusion that the far end of the cave was receding the more I swam towards it. At one moment I thought I saw a huge tortoise floating by ... I was almost afraid ... I swam furiously for about half an hour. Eventually, after an hour, I touched the edge. A small plateau beside a yawning hole – which went where? I have to admit that I was frightened ... I swam back, to find Tehura praying. I think there was irony in her smile as she asked me: 'Weren't you afraid?' Boldly, I replied, 'Frenchmen know no fear!'[2]

The light, it is true, plays tricks there. But the cave is, in fact, no more than fifty metres long, and it takes an Englishman two minutes to swim to the far end.

Gauguin, here as elsewhere, could not, it seems,

be trusted with the facts. He made things up. Whether it was to impress the public back in France, or simply to boost his own opinion of himself – who knows, and perhaps it does not matter. What is important to us is that this great storyteller was also a great artist: and the stories, the distortions, he introduced into his paintings were something of quite a different kind. The reason we value Gauguin's paintings is that then, by departing from the facts, he came closer to a deeper truth.

What was it Gauguin wanted to convey? What was it he believed? He believed that all human beings contain within themselves a savage soul – the soul of Eve: Eve innocent, before the Fall, without guile and therefore without guilt, but none the less a *pagan* Eve, natural, wilful, the mother and mistress of us all. He believed it because he had felt it in himself. Even before he left France for Tahiti,

he had painted his first 'Tahitian' picture – a soulful, primitive nude, posed in the Garden. That is what he had come to find.

But what were the facts? By the 1890s Tahiti had been spoiled. The women wore clothes; they hid their breasts in shame. They had lost touch with savage nature. Their ancestors were forgotten, the ancient pagan temples were in ruin.

What did Gauguin do? With the licence of every great artist, he meddled with the facts to get to the reality beneath. 'This world I am discovering is a Paradise, the outlines of which I have summarily sketched out.' But to make – or rather to remake – that paradise, he undressed his women, he replaced the idols they had lost, he *gave* them memories.

> I can understand Tehura, in whom her ancestors sleep and sometimes dream ... I strive to see and think through this child, and to find in her traces of the far away past which socially is dead indeed, but still persists in vague memories.[3]

August Strindberg wrote of Gauguin: he is 'a child taking his toys to pieces to make new ones'.[4] But what Gauguin was doing was the reverse, he was taking new toys to pieces to make old ones. He came to these islands to discover and represent human beings in a state of savage innocence, unspoiled by civilization. That is not what he found on the surface – the missionaries had been there before him – but it is what he revealed.

No great artist ever attempts merely to copy nature. In painting, drama, or literature the purpose of the work of art is not so much to *reproduce* the world as to *explain* it. The artist represents things not as they are but as they might be, if only we could see what lies within. So the artist idealizes, caricatures, distorts. What is the difference between a van Gogh chair and the chairs that we all know? Van Gogh was trying to tell us something about 'chairness'. Gauguin was trying to tell us something about 'humanness'. We live, as Plato said, in a world of shadows; the point of art – the point of philosophy – is to reveal the solid forms.

Gauguin was not, of course, the first – or last – to believe that to understand contemporary man we have to bring to light his savage origins. Nor was he the first to see the contradiction between human nature and an imposed veneer of civilization. In 1784 the French philosopher Denis Diderot had written a 'Supplement to the Voyage of Monsieur Bougainville', in which he discussed the lessons of Tahiti.

> Would you like to know the condensed history of almost all our present miseries? Here it is. There existed a natural man; an artificial man was introduced within this man; and within this cavern a civil war breaks out which lasts for life.
>   Weep, poor folk of Tahiti, weep! . . . One day you will know these Europeans better. One day they will return, with the crucifix in one hand and the dagger in the other to cut your throats or to force you to accept their customs and opinions; one day under their rule you will be almost as unhappy as they are.[5]

Diderot himself never set foot outside Europe, but like many of his generation he was profoundly influenced by the *idea* of Tahiti.

A century earlier the poet John Dryden had conjured up the image of the Noble Savage:[6]

> I am as free as nature first made man,
> Ere the base laws of servitude began,
> When wild in woods the noble savage ran.

But it was Diderot's friend and mentor, Jean-Jacques Rousseau, who had made the notion philosophically respectable. In France in the 1750s

Rousseau wrote his *Discourse on the Inequality of Man*, followed a few years later by the *Social Contract*. Its opening lines rang like a clarion call: 'Man was born free, and everywhere he is in chains.'

Rousseau pictured all men as having dwelt once in a state of nature, where all they needed or enjoyed was food, sleep and a woman – any woman. In this Eden-like existence a man had little to fear, because nobody envied him; he was not jealous, because one woman was as good as another; and he was not unhappy, because he had no ambition. It was the coming of civilization which wrecked it all.

Do you think, like GAUGUIN, that all HUMAN BEINGS contain a SAVAGE SOUL? ...

My dear chap. absolutely...

The first man who, having staked off a bit of land, said 'This is mine,' and found people stupid enough to believe him, was the true founder of civil society.[7]

But did this picture have any historical validity? Did Noble Savages exist? To Rousseau the question was an academic one. It was the *concept* of the noble savage that fired his imagination.

The state of nature may exist no longer, perhaps never existed, probably never will exist; [but it is something] of which it is necessary to have a just idea, in order to judge well our present state.[8]

Rousseau wanted a story – a creation myth of sorts – in the light of which people could assess the achievements and limits of European civilization. The story's value, indeed its claim to truth, lay in whether or not it worked to deepen people's understanding of their present state and future possibilities. The meaning of servitude lay in contrasting it with a hypothetical society where men were free. The meaning of the ceremony of marriage lay in contrasting it with a hypothetical state of nature where marriage was neither necessary nor desirable.

It would be odd to call Rousseau's book a work of art, but it was hardly a work of science, as most people understand the term. No one would have imagined that there could ever be an objective 'test' of Rousseau's story. Nor was there meant to be: like much philosophy, it was conceived as a thought-experiment about how things might be and what it would mean if they were.

Then, within twenty years, the travellers' tales began to come back from the South Seas. Here were the noble savages, the youth of the world! Diderot, in his imagination, interviewed an old man from Tahiti:

> We are innocent, we are happy ... Here everything belongs to everybody ... Our daughters and our wives are common to us all ... When we hunger, we have enough to eat; when we are cold we have wherewith to clothe us ... We have reduced the sum of our labours to the least possible, because nothing seems preferable to us to repose.[9]

To people who previously had taken Rousseau's fable only half-seriously, it must have seemed a miraculous confirmation. You guess at the existence of a planet, and lo and behold the astronomers fifty years later discover it. You guess at the existence of a state of nature, and lo the sailors return with the full story. Captain Cook even brought a savage called Omai home with him. Omai had lunch with Dr Johnson, who found him charming; he was introduced to King George, and said 'How do, King Tosh'.

But would it have made any difference to the impact of the *Social Contract* if Tahiti had never been discovered? No. The point about philosophi-

Alas-
poor HAMLET
I knew him well..

NAME DROPPER!

cal stories, like works of art, is that they help shape men's ideas. If the story turns out to have some kind of objective validity, that is an extraordinary – though unnecessary – bonus. If an explorer were to discover a woman with a Picasso face, or an archaeologist were to dig up the bones of a real historical Hamlet, would that make Picasso a greater painter, Shakespeare a greater playwright? No.

Is that then the difference between Art and Science? Science, you might think, has in the end to get things factually correct. If a scientist suggests that the earth is flat, and it turns out to be round, then the scientist had better try again. Logically, science and art are concerned with different kinds of truth. And yet that does not mean that scientists and artists are different kinds of people, or even that they think in different ways. The goal of both is always to go after the deeper structure, to reveal some hidden order beneath the surface of appearances. The scientist's strategy, just like that of the artist, is to consult first his own imagination: to guess what the answer might be.

The difference, and perhaps it is the only real difference, between art and science lies in the kind of probing and testing that goes on. Scientists live more dangerously than artists. If an artist does not satisfy his critics he can claim – often with justice – that the failure is theirs, that they have not understood him or that his work is not for them. But scientists cannot choose their 'audience'. A scientific theory must, eventually, be able to convince the whole community of scientific sceptics by standing up to every rational and factual objection thrown at it. But that comes later, if it ever does. The inspired guess, the hypothesis, comes first. And often the joy of discovery stops there.

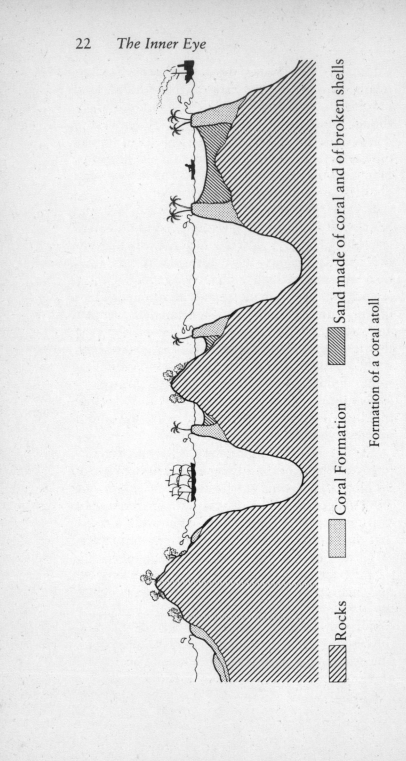

Rocks

Coral Formation

Sand made of coral and of broken shells

Formation of a coral atoll

Einstein himself never performed an experiment. With his Theory of Relativity, he imagined a new way of looking at the world. The key came to him unexpectedly, after years of bafflement, as he awoke one morning and sat up in bed. Keys either fit or they do not. Einstein knew straight away that his key did.

But, for me, it is Charles Darwin, not Einstein, who best illustrates the nature of scientific creativity. Darwin came to Tahiti in 1835, aboard His Majesty's Research Ship, *Beagle*. He was 26 years old.

From my earliest youth I had the strongest desire to understand or explain whatever I observed – that is, to group all facts under some general laws ... [There was an old stone in my home town of

GAUGUIN came here to PAINT and SLEEP with NATIVE WOMEN — and DARWIN came to look at CORAL ATOLLS and RESEARCH POLYPS ...

TAHITI

Shrewsbury, called the Bell-Stone.] Mr Cotton assured me there was no rock of the same kind nearer than Cumberland or Scotland, and he solemnly assured me the world would come to an end before anyone would be able to explain how this stone came where it now lay. This produced a deep impression on me, and I meditated over this wonderful stone.[10]

Darwin was someone who speculated about everything, took nothing for granted – even the very rock under his feet.

Tahiti, an extinct volcano, has sloping sides extending deep into the sea. Coral polyps – tiny sea anenome-like animals – grow profusely in the shallow fringing waters. They secrete a hard skeleton which masses to form coral rock, and round Tahiti this rock has formed a fringing reef. But close by is an island of a more surprising kind. From the peak of Tahiti you can just see the atoll of Tetiaroa. It is made *entirely* of coral – not just a hundred foot or so of it, but coral upon coral going down thousands of feet. The problem is that Tetiaroa is built up of coral *at depths at which coral cannot grow*. The existence of such atolls, Darwin wrote, 'is a wonder which does not at first strike the eye of the body, but, after reflection, the eye of reason.'[11]

Other scientists of his generation might simply have recorded their surprise and travelled on, but not Darwin. Hypotheses were his delight: 'I cannot resist forming one on every subject'. Suppose, he thought, that the earth's surface is continually changing: islands rise out of the sea, and *islands sink again*. What would happen to a volcanic island like Tahiti as it slowly sank, at a rate of perhaps a few inches a year? The coral would go on growing around the sides, supported at first by solid rock

but eventually only by the bank of previously accumulated coral. In time the original volcano might
disappear completely beneath the surface of the
sea. What would be left? An atoll like Tetiaroa.

This idea of Darwin's – which is almost certainly
correct – has been called since 'an exemplary scientific hypothesis'. But at the time, it was not a hypothesis for which Darwin himself had any
scientific evidence. It appealed to him, even
without evidence, because it was better than any
other theory that was going.

It may be asked whether I can offer any direct evidence ... but it must be born in mind how difficult it must ever be to detect a movement, the tendency of which is *to hide under water* the part affected ... I venture to defy anyone to explain it in any other manner.[12]

In fact, as Darwin revealed later, he thought up the whole theory on the west coast of South America, before he had even so much as seen a coral atoll.

Still, exemplary as it was, this story would now probably be no more than a footnote to scientific history, if Darwin had not gone on to apply his imagination to the solution of a much grander problem: that of the origin of species.

Most people now know the answer he came up with: species evolve by the process of natural selection. As the environment changes, and as new variations get thrown up, there is a continuing competition for survival. The fittest animals are those which bear most offspring. And it is they – or rather their genetic traits – which will be represented in succeeding generations. It is clear how the same mind was at work here: a mind fascinated by the idea of unseen processes. Species, like the earth's surface itself, are always changing. Everything is connected back in history. Species are like islands on the surface of time. He made the parallel explicit in his notebooks: 'The tree of life should perhaps be called the coral of life, base of branches dead so that passages cannot be seen.'[13]

The theory was beautifully worked out. But again, at the time Darwin devised it, he had extraordinarily little evidence. Indeed, it was not just a matter of his not having enough information: several of the 'facts' he did have actually seemed to work against him. Lord Kelvin, for example, had made some calculations on the age of the Earth, which showed that, at most, it was some hundreds of millions of years old. Yet Darwin's theory implied that the processes of change must have been continuing very much longer. We now know that Kelvin's calculations were in error but, at the time, Darwin had no way of refuting them. He could only trust his own inventor's sense of what the truth should be and if the apparent facts were frustrating or annoying, then he must hope the facts themselves would change. His theory was too good to be wrong.

'The *a priori* reasoning is so entirely satisfactory to me,' his elder brother said, 'that if the facts won't fit in, why so much the worse for the facts.'[14] Darwin himself would not publicly have gone so far. None the less he did perhaps have in his theory an *artistic faith* – the faith of which Paul Dirac was speaking when he said of Einstein: 'It is more important to have beauty in one's theory than to have it fit experiment.'[15] Like Gauguin painting his idealized Eve before he had set foot in Tahiti, like Rousseau dreaming up the Noble Savage from a Paris salon, Darwin *anticipated* nature.

Creative geniuses, Diderot wrote, are people whom nature has taken into her confidence so that they are able to 'smell out things still to be discovered, new experiments, unknown results'.[16] They imagine more than they have seen, but in doing that they do not so much create an imaginary world as glimpse the hidden order of the existing world.

Who are they, these geniuses? Look in a mirror. The trait is, I think, entirely commonplace. We all, every day of our lives, imagine more than we can see. We do so not as artists or as scientists but as ordinary social human beings. And we do it most impressively and most importantly when – almost without noticing it – we make imaginative guesses about the hidden contents of the human mind. I am by profession a psychologist, someone whose job it is to try to understand the behaviour and the minds of men and animals. But after twenty years, I have come to realize that the title is absurd. I *am* a psychologist – but so are all other human beings.

Why did he say that?
And in that tone of voice?
And so aggressive as well -
He might be SHY - or KIND - but
it's hard to tell if he uses
such LANGUAGE right at
the BEGINNING of the
RELATIONSHIP..
Hello!

We have only so much as to glance at another human being and we at once begin to read beneath the surface. We see there another conscious person, like ourselves. We see someone with human feelings, memories, desires. A mind potentially like ours. And yet, of course, human feelings are the one thing we do not 'see', any more than Darwin was able to see the hidden mountains underneath the ocean. What I *see* is her face, what I *smell out* is her inner feelings. It is that gift – the universal human gift of conscious insight – that I want to understand.

TWO
Natural Psychologists

Darwin's theory of organic evolution gave me a way of looking at the living world that I could not put away. Everything in nature can potentially be explained in Darwinian terms. Whenever we find anything in nature that is beautiful, well-formed, apparently designed for a purpose, we can guess that behind it lies the slow, halting process of natural selection. The shapes, the forms, the faculties of plants and animals have evolved only because they contribute in some way to biological survival. It is as true for the shape of the trees in the forest, as for the colours of a butterfly and for the hair on our own heads – and it ought to be true for our own *minds*. The minds of human beings are part of nature. We should ask: What are minds for? Why have they evolved in this way rather than another? Why have they evolved at all, instead of remaining quite unchanged?

In Darwin's words: 'He who understands *baboon* would do more toward metaphysics than John Locke.'[1] My chance to see our primate cousins' minds in operation came when, in 1971, I had the opportunity to work for three months among the mountain gorillas which live on the slopes of the Virunga volcanoes in Rwanda.

I had a particular job to do while I was there. A few weeks before, a family of gorillas had been killed by poachers. Eight bodies had been left lying in the forest, and they had been brought back to zoologist Dian Fossey's camp. Even in death gorillas are precious to science and it was important that these animals' skeletons – especially the skulls – should be measured and preserved. The carcases were rotting and full of worms. I boiled them in a kerosene tin to loosen the skin from the bones, then I reassembled the skeletons. At night I sat up measuring them. By day, however, I went out into the field to observe the living animals. I would get up with the sun, follow the gorillas' trail from their resting place the night before, and join them for the day's activity.

Gorillas seldom range more than a mile or so each day. They know their own territory well and seldom leave it – unless they have been scared by human poachers, or perhaps been upset by a hostile encounter with another group from the next valley. Typically, they live in family groups of about ten members led by one, or sometimes two, experienced males. Their daily routine is simple and predictable. They rise from their night nests not too early in the morning and feed for a while on vines, bamboo shoots or wild celery, before going off to some known patch where food is plentiful. They will stop for a rest in the sun to nap and chew things over, then travel a bit further, feed again, and then on to a suitable camp site where they construct nests of branches and leaves and settle down comfortably for the night. It is not a bad life. In fact it seems remarkably easy. Little to do, apparently, and little done but eat, sleep and play.

It seemed too easy. The more I observed them,

the more puzzled I became. Every evening I was handling and measuring the skulls of the members of a gorilla family much like those I was watching during the day – skulls which once housed gorilla brains, gorilla minds – and the first thing which impressed me was their size. A gorilla's brain is very large – not proportionately as large as a man's but larger relative to its body than any other land animal except the chimpanzee. Moreover, the left side of the brain appeared from my measurements to be larger than the right – a trait which in man is associated with the specialization of the brain for language. But to what use could the gorillas be putting those large brains?

Brains, you might think, are for solving problems. Gorillas ought, therefore, to be animals of very high intelligence. In fact, from tests on captive animals, we know they are. In the laboratory, psychologists have shown that gorillas – and equally chimpanzees – can do all sorts of extremely clever things: solve difficult conceptual puzzles, put things together in their heads, and even gain symbolic mastery over a machine. Not surprisingly, it has been taken for granted that the intelligence on display in the laboratory must also be being used in some way in the wild. Indeed it has been assumed that the problems the gorillas face in nature must be very like those they have to face in the laboratory, problems which require a practical solution: What will happen if I join these sticks together? How can I find my way from A to B? Where's my next meal coming from?

The reality I observed every day in the forest was, however, perplexingly different. There was no obvious sign of the gorillas using their intelligence to any practical advantage. Hard as I looked, I

I wish I knew what my BRAINS were for...

never saw them do anything that struck me as being clever, let alone any sign that they were having to solve difficult conceptual problems. Indeed, what problems were there? Why should they bother? Life seemed so simple. Food abundant and easy to gather – provided they knew where to find it. No real danger from predators – provided they knew how to avoid them. There was a paradox here, not just a psychological paradox, but a biological and evolutionary one. Darwin's theory suggests that little if anything exists in nature without a reason. Yet here apparently was an exception to the rule. The gorillas had more brain-power than they could ever need.

Suppose you found an animal with well-developed wings, and yet all your observations of it showed that the animal never used those wings. You would be surprised. What a waste! How out of line with the economy of nature! But you would not for that reason reject Darwin's theory. You would guess – or at least hope – that the error was your own, not evolution's. If the bird did not fly while you watched it, then perhaps it did fly *when you were not looking.* By the same token there must, I thought, be more to the gorillas' apparently uncomplicated lifestyle than I was seeing. Was there something going on, perhaps right before my eyes, which I was simply failing to pick up – or at least not recognizing as requiring high intelligence?

I tried to put myself in the gorillas' place, and to imagine what – if anything – might really tax their minds. As I did so I found myself thinking equally about myself. Where did *my* real problems lie? The fact was that I had come to Africa not primarily for scientific reasons, but to escape an impossible human situation back at home. My marriage had broken down; I was deeply involved in an on-off way with another woman; her marriage had broken down; parents, friends, a psychoanalyst were trying to help. My head (when I was not thinking about gorillas) was full of unresolved problems concerning my own social relationships. That was what I thought about by day and night, what filled my brain and presented me with a host of truly baffling questions. If I do this, what will *she* do? But suppose I did *that*, or if she did something else...? Suddenly I saw the animals with new eyes. I realized that, for them too, their problems were probably primarily *social* ones.

The reason why life in the forest seems to pose so few problems for these apes is precisely because the gorilla *family*, as a social unit, is so well adapted to it. An ape brought up under the care of others – protected while he is young, shown the ways of the forest – will not have much problem in coping with the outside world. Indeed even the practical problems will be taken care of. He will be shown how to do things. A gorilla infant does not have to discover what is good and bad to eat; his mother teaches him. A chimpanzee does not have to invent new foraging techniques; skills such as fishing for termites are passed on by tradition.

The problems of creating and maintaining such a stable social group are quite another matter. The social life of a gorilla may not, to an outside observer, look all that problematical, but that is only because the animals themselves are so accomplished at it. They know each other intimately, they know their place. None the less there *are* endless small disputes about social dominance, about who grooms who, about who should have first access to a favourite food, or sleep in the best site. Sometimes

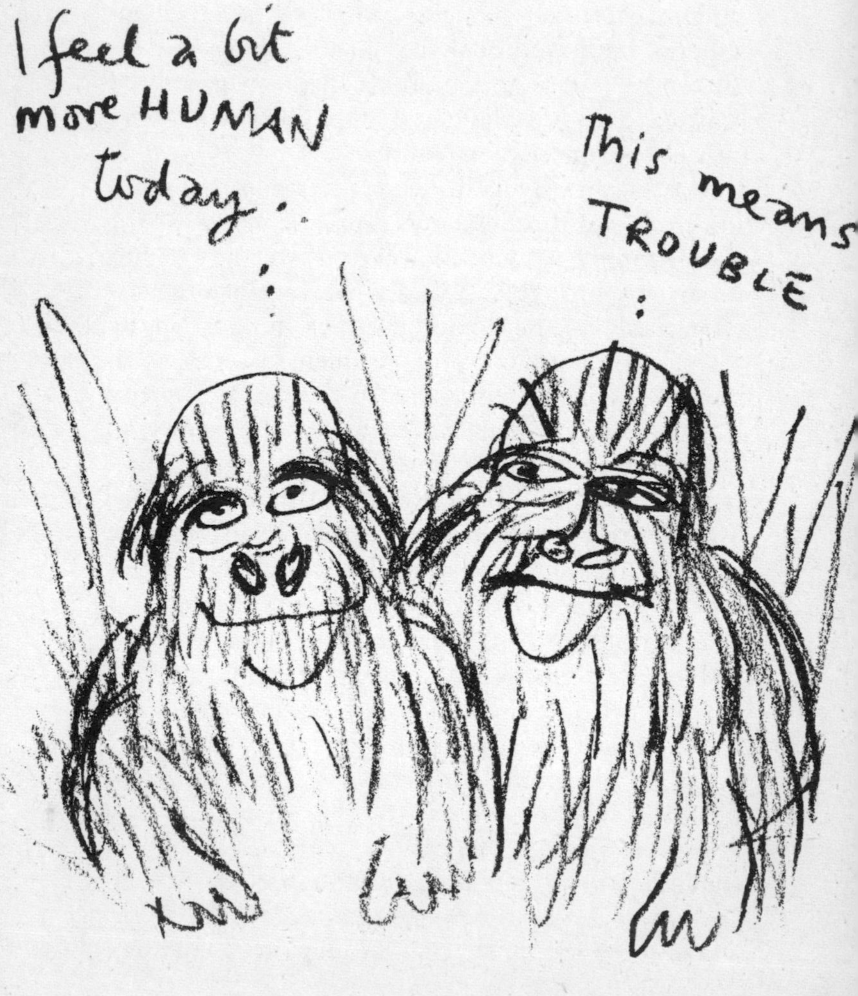
I feel a bit more HUMAN today.
This means TROUBLE

it is more serious: major disagreements about who should mate with who, about when a young male should be turned out of the family, or when and whether a strange female should be allowed to join them.

The major set-tos may not happen often, but when they do they can be literally a matter of life and death. Most silverback gorillas bear scars received in brutal fights with other males. Most older females have probably lost at least one baby through infanticide. The forest may not present any great problems to gorillas, but the behaviour of other gorillas can and does. The intelligence required to survive socially is something of quite a different order to that needed to cope with the material world.

Social intelligence is clearly the key to the great apes' biological success. It is in dealing with each other that these animals have to think, remember, calculate, and weigh things up inside their heads. And social intelligence requires every ounce of brain power they have got.

After three months I had to return home. But I was returning now with the germ of an idea: the idea of what I came to call *natural psychology*. Gorillas and chimps, I thought, had evolved to be psychologists by nature. They were using their brains – their senses, their memories, their abstract intellectual skills – at their limits when handling their relationships with one another.

Back in Cambridge I was plunged straight into the thick of my own human relationships. Inevitably the thought occurred to me: if the gorillas I had been watching were spending most of their time worrying about their social relationships, and if the gorilla's brain had evolved largely for the purpose of doing that worrying, then might that not be what my brain – and other people's brains – were for as well?

Of course, no one would pretend that the life of gorillas has very much in common with the life of human beings. We possess powers of language, creativity and self-awareness that, so far as we know, no other animal possesses; and our human societies are infinitely richer, more stable and more psychologically demanding than anything which exists elsewhere in nature. But the gorillas' strategy for survival – the strategy of relying on the social group to provide both a protective mafia and a kind of polytechnic school – is one we share. Indeed it is one which we human beings have made the keystone of our whole existence. Nowhere on earth can human beings survive outside society. And consequently nowhere on earth can human beings survive without a deep sensitivity to and understanding of their fellow creatures.

Did people, too, then evolve to be psychologists by nature? Is that what makes our families and communities work? Has that been the prime mover behind the evolution of *our* brains and *our* intelligence? If so, it would mean that almost all the earlier theories of human evolution had got it upside down. Fifteen years ago, nothing in the textbooks about human evolution referred to man's need to do psychology: the talk was all of toolmaking, spear-throwing and fire-lighting – practical rather than social intelligence.

In 1976 I went to visit Richard Leakey and Glyn Isaac at the site in Northern Kenya where they and their team, by examining the fossil record, had been slowly uncovering man's early history. During the month I was there, Leakey unearthed one of the

oldest and most complete of the man-ape skulls, dating from about one-and-a-half million years ago. I remember the touch of that skull, and it made me wonder with a new intensity about what *kind* of a person — emotionally and psychologically — he could have been. His brain was already twice the size of a gorilla's. His ancestors some millions of years earlier had made the break with the great apes. Why? What pressures or opportunities were the ancestors of human beings responding to?

Africa about twenty million years ago was a much lusher place than it is now. Warm, steaming forests covered the continent, and in those forests lived the common ancestor of modern apes and man — a fruit-eating, tree-dwelling animal about the size of a baboon. Then the climate changed and the forests began to thin out and retreat. Our ancestors came down on to the forest floor; they grew bigger and larger-brained — and almost certainly at that point began to be more socially dependent, with a family structure something like that of the modern chimpanzee.

The weather cooled further; areas of sparsely-treed grassland were developing. A new ecological niche was becoming available which was perhaps tempting to those early apes, but too risky and difficult, too technically demanding to lure them from their traditional haven in the trees. To exploit this new niche a new 'subsistence technology' would have to be developed. It would require a close knowledge of the plants and animals, it would require tools, weapons, a system of sharing. It would require, in short, something approaching a human culture — and our chimpanzee-like ancestors were not yet capable of that. Clever and highly social as they were, I believe they were still incapable of maintaining the intimate long-term social relationships on which human culture depends.

Then, around six million years ago, the first experiment in human social life seems to have been made. While one group of apes – the ancestors of today's gorillas and chimpanzees – stayed behind, another group – the animals from which we are descended – took to the field. It was the parting of the ways. A new line of man-like apes emerged, with the bodies, and more importantly the minds, that would allow them to survive and flourish as hunters and gatherers on the savannah.

It has been argued that the mark of the first man-like ape was the ability to walk on his hind legs, or to eat and digest a wider range of grassland food, or to relate his fingers to his thumb. All those were certainly important. But the more I learned of the discoveries Glyn Isaac was making about early social life, the more convinced I was that the answer lay elsewhere. Not fingers to thumb, but person to person. The real mark of a man-like ape would have been his ability to manipulate and relate himself – in human ways – to the other apes around him. We cannot tell when these new-found social skills began to bear real fruit, but there is sufficient archaeological evidence to suggest that by two million years ago the fundamental pattern of human social living had already been laid down. Human beings were living in small communal groups, centred round a home base. There was division of labour, and sharing of food. Sexual relationships were probably monogamous and long-lasting. Both mother and father helped rear the children. Subsistence skills were the property of the community, and passed on by tradition. Already by that

We have taken
MILLIONS of years to
evolve from APES
and here you
are-
STILL ACTING
Like a GORILLA-
(TUT-TUT)

stage the social structure was so far in advance of anything that exists among the other apes, that it implies a quantum leap in the underlying *psychological* skills of the community.

Although we can no longer have any direct evidence of how it worked there exist today people whose lives provide a model. The Bushmen of the Kalahari may be biologically modern, but in many respects their lifestyle has not changed substantially in the last million years. We can still see just how far the success of such a hunter-gatherer community depends on the psychological skills of its individual members. Every aspect of such people's lives is socially conditioned. All their subsistence techniques – all they know of hunting, cooking, weaving, healing, the cycle of the seasons, the cycle of their lives – is learned through the social interaction of one person with another. Their lives are based on trust, reciprocity, division of labour between the sexes and between generations.

But at what cost do the individuals buy in to this typically human, if primitive, community? They do so by eternal psychological vigilance. They may spend time apparently doing nothing, passing time in idle gossip. But this time spent socializing is as crucial to their survival as any time spent hunting or gathering in the field. For it is round the camp fire or lying out in the sun that the social backbone of Bushman society is laid down and, if necessary, repaired: friendships are established, problems talked out, plans hatched, love affairs commented on. Beneath the surface there are, as everywhere with human beings, petty jealousies, domestic squabbles, suspicions of favouritism, infidelity. Yet seldom, if ever, do social disputes get out of hand. The social system works. But it works only because these people are, like all human beings, supremely good at understanding one another. They come of a long, long line of natural psychologists whose brains and minds have been slowly shaped by evolution. Quite simply, those for whom it did *not* work were extinguished: they had fewer children and had less to give them – and they are no longer around today.

Yet if that was the lifestyle of our ancestors – if it worked so well – what led to the abandonment of hunting and gathering? What, after several million years, set human beings on the march again, on the path to what we now call 'civilization'?

It involved such a small shift in technique, and it happened so recently, that the answer still takes me by surprise. It is that, little more than 10,000 years ago, one branch of the human family invented *agriculture*. Instead of gathering wild plants they sowed them; instead of hunting wild animals they farmed and bred them. And with agriculture came settlement, specialization, surplus wealth, population growth, cities, politics and kings.

The larval stage of human development was over. Suddenly human culture chrysalized, to emerge as the butterfly of civilized society. Society became caught up in the winds of change: blown by the seemingly impersonal forces of money, trade, science, religion, war. But were the human beings at the centre of it a new breed of people? Did they lose their age-old bushman dependence on human interaction? No. Historians may describe these impersonal forces as they will. The fact remains that there are *no* impersonal forces in human society: there is not a single significant event that has not been shaped by individual human minds interacting with other human minds. The history of human

If only I could UNDERSTAND
his INNER FEELINGS we could
RELATE and join FORCES
and FORM GROUPS and
INVENT AGRICULTURE
and CROPS and BARTER and
MONEY and POLITICS
and GOVERNMENTS
and . . .
on second thoughts—
better LEAVE
well
alone . . .
. . . .

If we are to SURVIVE our society needs to develop 'THE RELATIONSHIP' - we must interact MORE with our NEIGHBOURS.. we must LEARN how they FEEL etc..
?

society over the last few thousand years is the history of what people have *said* to each other, what they have *thought* of each other, of rivalries, friendships, personal and national ambitions. If that is true for political, religious, and cultural change, it is just as true for the material trends within society. Technological progress does not just happen. It lifts off from a bed of human social interaction.

There is a story told that when the Americans and the Russians arrived simultaneously on the surface of the moon, they were surprised to be greeted by a smiling Chinese peasant. 'How did you do it?' they asked. 'Oh,' said the Chinaman, 'it wasn't difficult. Lee Ho stood on Kow Loon's shoulders, Kow Loon stood on Tu Ming's – and we went on from there.' The story has a deeper truth to it. We may send rockets into space. But those rockets do no more than hitch-hike on the backs of individual human beings.

Being human ourselves, we take it all for granted, as a bird no doubt takes for granted its ability to fly. *We underestimate ourselves.* A marriage, a friendship, a workplace partnership, indeed almost every relationship we embark on, testifies to our remarkable human social skills. No animals make friends or work together at the level human beings do. No animal could sustain a human marriage. None would dare.

> His love for Tereza was beautiful, but it was also tiring: he had constantly to hide things from her, sham, dissemble, make amends, buck her up, calm her down, give her evidence of his feelings, play the defendant to her jealousy, her suffering and her dreams, feel guilty, make excuses and apologies...

This extract is from a book called *The Unbearable Lightness of Being*, by Milan Kundera.[2] That will do. Small wonder human beings have evolved to be such remarkable psychological survivors, when for the last six million years their heavy task has been *to read the minds of other human beings*.

Yet *how* do we do it? What do we mean when we talk of 'psychological insight' or of our ability to 'put ourselves in someone else's place'? Human beings, for all their humanness, are essentially immensely complicated biological machines; and human behaviour is the product of the electrical and chemical events that go on in human brains. When we say 'I know what it's like to be another person', we are making a strange and a mysterious claim. For we are saying in effect that we have an understanding of the human brain far superior to anything which scientific psychology yet has to offer.

None of us has 'X-ray eyes'. What do we have?

THREE
The Ghost in the Machine

Some years ago there was a game in fashion in which people were given the answer to an unasked question, and invited to guess what the question might have been. For example, to the answer 'Dr Livingstone I presume', the question might be 'What is your full name, Dr Presume?'; or to the answer '9 W' the question might be 'Does your name begin with a V, Herr Wittgenstein?' For a long time I puzzled with the answer 'consciousness' ... Consciousness is such an ineluctable presence in our lives. And yet it is not clear that consciousness is the *answer* to anything at all.

By consciousness I mean the inner picture we each have of what it is like to be ourselves – self-awareness: the presence in each of us of a spirit, (self, soul...) which we call 'I'. It's 'I' who have thoughts and feelings, sensations, memories, desires. It's 'I' who am conscious of my own existence and my continuity in time. 'I' who am, in short, the very essence of a human being.

But what is going on? This presence called 'I' has no separate reality – separate, that is, from the activity of my own brain. Everything which I am consciously aware of corresponds in one way or another to a brain state. 'Feeling hungry' is a state of my brain; 'seeing red' is a state of my brain; even my notion of 'being me' must be a brain state. But then why could not all this stuff go on inside my head *without my being consciously aware of it*? What is consciousness *doing*? What *difference* does it make to any of our lives?

There are three possibilities which might more or less make sense. (*1*) Consciousness might be making all the difference in the world: it might be a necessary precondition of all intelligent and purposive behaviour, both in man and animals. (*2*) Consciousness might be making no difference whatsoever: it might be a purely accidental feature, which happens sometimes (not always?) to be present in some (but not all?) animals and has no influence upon the way they act. (*3*) Consciousness might, for those animals which have it, be making the difference between success and failure *in some particular compartment of their lives*.

I will not hide that I think this third possibility the most interesting – and the most likely. But to get to it, we have to dispose of the first two.

Of the three possibilities, common sense must, initially, back the first. In our own lives, it seems that consciousness makes all the difference. For most people, most of the time, there seem in fact to be only two possible states of being: either we are alive, alert and conscious with it, or we are flat on our backs, inert and unconscious. When we 'lose' consciousness we lose touch with the world. And if *that* is the difference between being conscious and unconscious, are there really any further questions to be asked?

If that was all there was to it, we would, indeed, not have to search much further. But the problem is that while experience tells us one thing, logic tells us something else. Experience says that whenever a man is up and about he *must* be conscious and aware of his own inner thoughts and feelings. But logic says: Hold on a minute. How do you know? Is there any reason in principle why an animal, or even a human being, could not be behaviourally alert and yet still be 'unconscious', in this important sense: that he is still quite unaware of what is going on inside his mind? The mere fact that a man happens to be on his feet and apparently behaving quite normally, does not prove anything. How do we know he is not some kind of biological robot – that the whole performance is not some kind of bizarre mechanical charade?

It is the analogy with machines which ought to set us wondering. Many machines behave in ways which, if they were human, would suggest that they had conscious mental states. An aeroplane on auto-pilot, for example, can fly itself. It responds to external 'sensory' information, it makes 'decisions' about where to fly, it 'communicates' with other aeroplanes. It even shows some kinds of emotional behaviour – it knows when it is 'hungry' for fuel, it can sense 'danger', it can react adaptively to 'pain' or 'injury'. In some ways it is as intelligent and pur-posive as many animals.

Three hundred years ago, it was just such an ana-logy which led René Descartes to deny the existence of consciousness in any animal other than man. Almost every action of an animal could, he claimed (and he could not in the seventeenth century have known how true this claim might become), be simulated by an inanimate machine. Imagine a machine equipped with sophisticated sensors for sound, light, temperature and so on, and a complex mechanical brain controlling its behaviour. It could have instincts. It could learn, remember, make predictions, take decisions.

> Nor will this seem in any way strange to those who know the different kinds of *automata*, or moving machines the industry of men can fabricate. If there were such machines which had the organs and appearance of a monkey or some other animal, we should have no way of recognizing that they were not entirely of the same nature as the animal.[1]

The extension of Descartes' argument was obvious: if animals *could* be unconscious automata, then for all he knew — and perhaps that was all he could know — animals *were*. Indeed, 'there is nothing which leads weak minds further astray than to imagine that the souls of animals are of the same nature as ours'.

Descartes' logic was good. But to many people, then as now, his conclusion when applied to animals in general seemed ethically disturbing. Machines might indeed resemble animals, animals might resemble machines. But surely only the cold logic of a philosopher could ignore the fact that machines are by definition dead, and animals alive. In 1648, the Englishman Henry More wrote to Descartes:

> There is nothing in your opinions which so disgusts me, so far as I have any kindness or gentleness, as the murderous view you put forward which snatches away life and sensibility from all the animals.[2]

Look how even a fly will struggle. Can anyone honestly believe that in some sense the fly is not feeling trapped and terrified? Descartes could. 'We can certainly conceive a machine so constructed that ... it may cry out that it is being hurt.' And why indeed should not a fly be such a machine?

Yet most of us naturally resist such an idea. As human beings we are inclined always to be generous and to see evidence of consciousness even when there is nothing to confirm it. We ask ourselves what it would *feel* like to be a fly or a lion or a baboon, supposing *we* were them. But Descartes was clear: it is only human sentimentality, and the lack of a philosophical training, which leads us to project our own feelings on to animals. 'If a lion could talk,' Wittgenstein wrote, 'we should not understand him.' Descartes' view on this point was much more radical. If a lion could talk, he would not, *when it comes to feelings*, have anything to say.

Descartes said animals had NO SOULS.

So what – philosophers can't grow their own COATS.

Descartes, by common judgement, was going too far. Maybe some other animals do not have the fully developed consciousness that we do. But is it really possible that no other animals have any consciousness at all? What about the simple facts of *perception*: seeing, hearing, touching? If Descartes is right, we should have to accept that animals do not even have sensations anything like ours – that they see without really 'seeing', hear without 'hearing', even hurt without feeling any pain. To be fair to him, he was quite consistent on this point. Animals do not, he thought, even see as we do, 'that is, being aware, or thinking that we see'.[3] When a sheep flees from a wolf, he said, the sheep is responding mechanically to the light reflected from the wolf's body, without consciousness having anything to do with it.

This idea of perception *sans* sensation may seem quite preposterous (a recent book on Descartes describes it as one of his more elementary mistakes). Yet it is an idea which recent scientific evidence requires us to take seriously. There is increasing evidence that the higher animals, including human beings, can in fact show the behaviour of perceiving without being consciously aware of what they are doing.

In Cambridge in the 1960s I became involved in an experiment which quite shook me up, and made me take nothing in this area for granted any more. There was a monkey called Helen in the laboratory who, as part of a study of the effects of brain damage in human beings, had undergone an operation which removed the visual cortex of her brain. I took up her case and worked with her for seven years, attempting to teach a 'blind' monkey to see.

At first, the operation left her unable to use her

eyes in any worthwhile way. She simply stopped bothering to look at things, as if she herself had no reason to believe that she could see. Yet, although her cortex was gone, the lower visual centres of her brain were still intact, and it was conceivable – to me, though not of course to her – that she might possess some residual capacity for vision of which she herself was unaware. I coaxed her and encouraged her, I played with her and took her for walks in the fields near the laboratory. I tried in every way to persuade her that she was *not* blind. Before six months were up it became apparent that a kind of miracle was happening: Helen, ever so slowly, was starting to use her eyes again. She improved so greatly over the next few years that eventually she could move deftly through a room full of obstacles and pick up tiny scraps of chocolate from the floor. To a stranger she would have appeared to be quite normal. But I was sure that she was *not* normal. I knew her too well, knew how much effort her recovery had cost her, and how bewildered she sometimes seemed to be. It was as though eyesight now had an entirely different meaning to her. Perhaps, I thought, in one sense it did not mean anything at all.

No one could be certain what was happening. To find out we would need evidence from human beings, and at that time there were no human cases comparable. Indeed what evidence there was suggested that people with similar brain damage would *not* recover vision. I wrote in 1972:

When people suffer extensive damage to the visual cortex it is said that their blindness is total and permanent. Perhaps with a more flexible definition of vision, it will yet be discovered that there is more to seeing than has so far met either the clinician's or the patient's eye.[4]

As it turned out, it was not so much a more flexible definition which was needed as a more flexible questioning of human patients by their doctors. In fact, within a few years, the first case was discovered of a condition which Larry Weiskrantz has called 'blindsight'.

Blindsight is seeing without knowing that you can see; unconscious vision; seeing things which to your conscious mind are quite invisible. In 1974 a patient, known by the initials D.B., was examined by Professor Weiskrantz and his colleagues at the National Hospital in London.[5] D.B. had recently undergone surgery to remove a growth at the back of his brain – an operation which meant the excision of the entire primary visual cortex on the right-hand side. The effect of the lesion was, as predicted from earlier clinical studies, that D.B. became blind in the left side of his field of vision. When, for example, he looked straight ahead he could not (with either eye) see anything to the left of his nose. Or so it seemed, both to D.B. himself and to the doctors who first tested his vision by asking him to tell them whether he could see a light going on or off in different parts of the field.

Weiskrantz, however, decided not to accept D.B.'s self-professed blindness at face value. There was no question that D.B. was genuinely unaware of seeing anything in the blind half of his field; but was it possible that his brain none the less was still receiving and processing the visual information? What would happen if he could be persuaded to discount his own conscious opinion?

Weiskrantz asked D.B. to forget for a moment

that he was blind, and to 'guess' at what he might be seeing *if* he could see. To D.B.'s own amazement, it turned out that he could do it. He could locate an object accurately in his blind field, and he could even guess certain aspects of its shape. Yet all the while he denied any conscious awareness.

Other cases of human 'blindsight' have now been described. Unconscious vision appears to be a clinical reality. In fact, there is evidence not only for unconscious vision, but for unconscious *touch* as well. A recent report describes a patient who was quite unaware of any feeling in her hand, but who could still 'guess' correctly which of her fingers was being touched. True enough, such cases always involve patients with brain damage, and this evidence cannot show that there are animals or people who, in perfect health, *naturally* perceive things without being aware of what is happening. What it does show, however, more dramatically than any logical argument could, is that Descartes might in principle have been correct. Consciousness, it seems, is not necessary to perception. Not only animals, but human beings themselves, can function without it, which opens up a huge range of possibilities. For if we can *perceive* without being conscious of any accompanying sensations, why should we not *think* without being conscious of our thoughts, *act* without being conscious of our own intentions, even *be ourselves* without, in any real sense, feeling we exist?

Consciousness is so central to our whole conception of the world – even to thinking about the problem in the first place – that the idea of generalized unconsciousness is certainly not easy to take in. Yet perhaps there are hints of what life without consciousness could mean. In the laboratory, psychologists have shown how it is possible for ordinary people to be influenced by subliminal events (below the threshold of awareness), or act on information they think they have forgotten, or solve problems – crossword puzzles, say – without knowing how they do it. Many of us have had the experience of driving a car from A to B, without remembering any details of the route, let alone the hundreds of gear-changes, and so on, we made along the way. Some of us may have walked in our sleep, and even perhaps held a simple conversation without waking up. If Freud was right, what about the ever-present influence of our subconscious minds? Much of our everyday lives may be directed by subconscious emotions we do not – and cannot – bring to conscious awareness. Someone may behave as if they are in love and yet deny it, or be influenced by terrible memories that cannot be recalled. But, if that is so, if human beings do sometimes, as it were, go on to 'autopilot', if much of behaviour, and perhaps in principle all of it, could occur unconsciously, what *is* consciousness doing?

Consciousness is clearly not essential to *every* aspect of our lives. Is it possible then that it is not needed at all? What about the second possibility I raised at the beginning of this chapter, that consciousness might be making no difference whatsoever?

The opinion that consciousness is indeed an 'epiphenomenon' – an accompanying event outside the chain of causation – has a distinguished pedigree. Charles Darwin's friend and disciple, T. H. Huxley, suggested the now famous analogy that consciousness is 'simply a collateral product, as completely without any power as the steam-whistle which accompanies the work of a locomotive is without influence on its machinery'.[6] Consciousness, he thought, was simply the noise of the brain's engine at work, huffing and puffing as it went about the business of processing the information which controls behaviour.

This simple analogy will not stand up, however, especially in the face of the evidence we have just been examining. If brains cannot help whistling a conscious tune, we should expect them to whistle all the time, and they do not. The human brain does not 'whistle', for example, when a blindsight-patient sees something in his blind field. It does not 'whistle' when a person is sleep-walking. For that matter it does not 'whistle' when it is carrying out the elaborate (in terms of information processing) task of running the vegetative systems of the body – temperature control, digestion, respiration, and so on.

There is, however, an alternative way of looking at Huxley's steam-whistle analogy. A locomotive whistles as it goes along simply as a result of steam escaping from its valves; but it may also have a polished-brass whistle attached to it, which sometimes sounds and sometimes doesn't. When the whistle blows, it does usually have some kind of higher purpose to it – though it still has no effect upon the locomotive's course.

This picture of consciousness is certainly closer to Descartes'; and indeed it may at one time have been close to Darwin's own. 'The soul,' Darwin wrote in one of his early notebooks, 'by the consent of all is superadded.'[7] Not only superadded but, by implication, in some way super-natural: a decorative addendum which blows off now and then (in our own case apparently quite frequently), but normally has no influence upon our natural lives. 'Animals', Darwin noted to himself in 1838, 'not got it'. It would have been unlike Darwin to have stayed with such a view, and he did not. 'Psychology', he later wrote, 'will be based on a new foundation, that of the necessary acquirement of each mental power by gradation.'[8] He himself never specifically tackled the problem of the 'necessity' of consciousness, but others soon raised the obvious Darwinian objection to the steam-whistle analogy in any of its varied forms. Lloyd Morgan, for example, in 1908:

> It is nothing less than pure assumption to say that consciousness, which is admitted to be present, has practically no effect whatever upon the behaviour. And we must ask any evolutionist who accepts this conclusion, how he accounts on evolutionary grounds for the existence of a useless adjunct to a neural process.[9]

Suppose – just suppose – that consciousness as we know it in human beings is indeed a product of natural evolution. Suppose our ability to look in upon ourselves and examine our own minds at work is as much a part of human biology as our ability to walk upright or to perceive the outside world. Once upon a time there were animals – our own ancestors presumably – who could not do it. They gave rise to descendants who *could*. Why should those conscious descendants have been selected in the course of evolution? In so far as Darwin's own theory of selection holds, there can be one answer and one answer only. Like every other natural faculty and structure, consciousness must have come into being because it conferred some kind of biological advantage on those creatures that possessed it. In some particular area of their lives, conscious human beings must have been able to do something which their unconscious forebears couldn't; something which, in competition with other members of their species, distinctly improved their chances of survival – and so of passing on the underlying genetic trait for consciousness to the next generation.

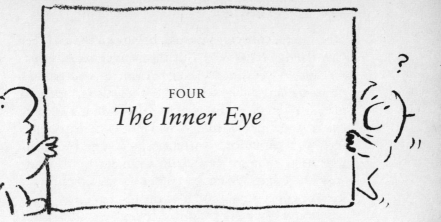

FOUR

The Inner Eye

If consciousness is the answer to anything at all, it must be the answer to a biological challenge which human beings – perhaps human beings alone – have had to meet. Could that challenge lie in the human need to understand, respond to and manipulate the behaviour of other human beings?

Such a solution now seems obvious, but I confess I did not get there straightaway. Indeed my first thought, as I hinted earlier, was that the key to our human ability to do 'natural psychology' must lie simply in our exceptional intelligence. We human beings can reason, calculate, remember as no other animals on earth. We have a fine eye for detail, and are good at discerning patterns. Given those analytic skills, and given the boundless opportunities we have for observing other people, why should we not learn to read people's behaviour in much the same way that we learn to read most other things in our environment: simply by piecing together the evidence we see before our eyes?

There is no question that we can and do learn a lot just by intelligent observation of what goes on around us. But I no longer believe that intelligence alone could ever be enough. It is one thing to notice the external facts, but it is quite another to read

beneath the surface and make sense of what we see.
Yet to make sense of it is precisely what we have to
do. When we watch the behaviour of our fellow
human beings, wc seldom, if ever, see merely a
mosaic of incidental acts: we see beneath it a deeper
causal structure – the hidden presence of plans,
intentions, emotions, memories, etc. – and it is on
that basis that we can claim to understand what
they are doing. We have in other words a picture, a
kind of conceptual model of the human mind, and
we should not be natural psychologists without it.

But the question is, where could such a model
come from? A model of the human mind must be,
in effect, a model of the human brain: and the
human brain is unimaginably complex – probably
the most complex mechanism in the universe. Is it
really at all likely that any ordinary person could
build up a model of the brain just by intelligent
external observation of how human beings behave?
Would anyone ever have the time, the patience or
indeed the scientific genius that would undoubtedly
be required?

Early this century a school of 'scientific psychology' came into being, whose hope was that human
behaviour *could* be made sense of entirely from
outside. The way forward, it was thought by the so-
called behaviourist psychologists, was to make
endless careful records of how people and animals
respond to external stimuli under carefully controlled laboratory conditions. The great thing was
strict objectivity: deliberately to avoid contaminat-
ing the results with any opinions and insights the
subjects themselves might want to offer. Thus J. B.
Watson, the founder of behaviourism in America,
in 1928:

The behaviourist sweeps aside all medieval conceptions. He drops from his scientific vocabulary all subjective terms such as sensation, perception, image, desire, and even thinking and emotion.[1]

Or B. F. Skinner, fifty years later:

> We seem to have a kind of inside information about our behaviour – *we* have feelings about it. And what a diversion they have proved to be! ... Feelings have proved to be one of the most fascinating attractions along the path of dalliance.[2]

Their conviction was that from the observational data alone it should be possible to construct theoretical models of the internal mechanism which controls behaviour: models which would finally account for everything which could be seen from the outside.

As a scientific attempt to understand behaviour, the behaviourist's approach was impeccable in intention and design. The problem, quite simply, was that it didn't work. After decades of intensive investigation and experiment, their picture of human – or for that matter animal – behaviour turned out to be astonishingly limited. That was not because the behaviourists were stupid; not because they could not make sufficient observations; not even because human behaviour is altogether inexplicable or lawless. Human behaviour does conform to certain – very special – laws. As a matter of fact you and I already know them, and use them all the time. But the lesson of behaviourism is clear: to discover these laws *from the outside* is a mammoth and almost hopeless task. It is far beyond science, and it would certainly be far beyond ordinary people – *if* that was what they had to do. But *we*, as Skinner said, 'have feelings' – and the irony is, as I now realize, that in dismissing these feelings as if they were a kind of scientific nuisance, the behaviourists were dismissing the most powerful tool imaginable for making sense of human lives.

Let's start with how we understand our own behaviour. I sit in the bath, say, at the end of a long day. Why am I there? Because I feel like having a relaxing soak. I turn on the hot tap. Why do I do that? Because I have no *wish* to get out yet, and I was beginning to feel cold. I start humming a tune which I remember hearing on the radio. I feel rather pleased with the sound of my own voice. I realize time's getting on, and think to myself I'd better get dressed and make the difficult phone call I've been dreading. I know I should have rung her earlier, but I didn't have the courage. Anyhow I can't find any soap ... and so on.

This situation is hardly, by the standards of human life, a complicated one. Yet even there in the bath the whole meaning of my behaviour would be quite obscure to anyone – including me – who did not have access, direct or indirect, to what I can observe going on inside myself. It is as if I, like every other human being, possess a kind of 'inner eye', which looks in on my brain and tells me why and how I'm acting in the way I am – providing me with what amounts to a plain man's guide to my own mind.

Imagine first the case of an animal that does not have an inner eye. It has sense organs which monitor the outside world, limbs which allow it to operate in and on its environment, and at the centre a sophisticated information-processor and decision-

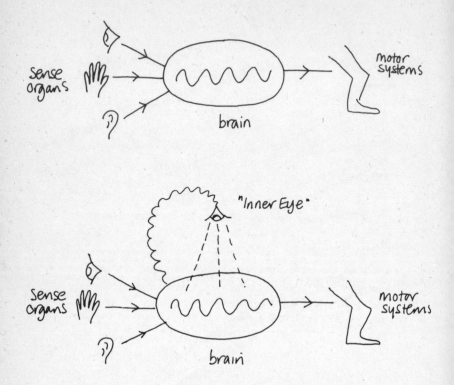

maker. But it has no insight into anything which is happening inside its brain. It is, in short, an unconscious Cartesian machine.

Now imagine that at some time in history a new kind of sense organ evolves, the inner eye whose field of view is not the outside world but the brain itself. Like other sense organs, the inner eye provides a picture of its information field that is partial and selective; but equally like other sense organs it has been designed by evolution so that its picture is a useful one, a 'user-friendly' description which tells the subject just so much as he requires to know in a form that he is predisposed to understand –

allowing him by a kind of magical translation to see his own brain-states as conscious states of mind.

If we compare these two at a purely behavioural level the unconscious and the conscious animal might be in most ways indistinguishable. Both could be highly intelligent; both might show emotional behaviour, moods, passions and so on. But while for the unconscious animal, the behaviour would just happen as if its brain were effectively on auto-pilot, for the conscious one every intelligent action would be accompanied by the *awareness* of the thought processes involved, every perception by an accompanying sensation, every emotion by a feeling.

Suppose that is indeed what *consciousness* amounts to, and that we human beings are the only animals in nature to have evolved this kind of inner eye. What would it mean for our ability to do psychology?

To begin with, it would mean that each individual human being would have almost literally a headstart in reading his own mind. No more fussing about like a behaviourist psychologist with 'intelligent guesses' about what lies behind our own behaviour. We would know immediately where the deeper explanation lies – in our own brain-states, which our inner eye reveals. But in practice it would mean very much more: for the explanation we have of our own behaviour could then form the basis for explaining *other people's*, too. We could, in effect, imagine what it's like to be them, because we know what it's like to be ourselves.

Here is an analogy. I live in a house on Chalcot Square. All round the square are other similar houses, into most of which I have never been. But I have no trouble in 'reading' what happens in those other houses on the basis of what I already know about my own. When, for example, I see smoke coming from a chimney I make sense of it in terms of what I know of the fire in my own hearth; when I see a light go on in a window, I make sense of it in terms of what I know of the effect of flicking a light switch in my own room; when I see someone appear first at a downstairs window, then an up-stairs one, I make sense of it in terms of my experience of mounting my own stairs. Then why not the same with other *people*, whose *minds* I have never been inside? Why should I not make sense of their behaviour by projecting what I know about *my* mind into *them*. The philosopher Thomas Hobbes stated the principle quite clearly:

> Given the similitude of the thoughts and passions of one man to the thoughts and passions of another, whosoever looketh into himself and considereth what he doth when he does think, opine, reason, hope, fear, &c., and upon what grounds, he shall thereby read and know what are the thoughts and passions of all other men upon the like occasions.[3]

I asked where our model of behaviour comes from. The answer is that, once we human beings evolved this inner eye, the model could be based directly on ourselves.

But there is perhaps a problem. How can we ever be certain that there is truly, as Hobbes put it, any similitude between our minds and other people's? Wittgenstein had a very different view of it. Suppose, he said, that everyone has a box with something in it. Let's call this thing a 'beetle'. 'No one can look into anyone else's box, and everyone says he knows what a beetle is only by looking at *his* beetle ... It would be quite possible for everyone to have something different in his box ... the box might even be empty.'[4]

Philosophically, the objection certainly has substance. Strictly speaking we have no hard evidence that any of our guesses about the inner life of other people are correct. Indeed Nature might have played a dreadful trick on us and built every human being according to a different plan. It is not just that the phenomenology of conscious experience might differ from one person to another: what I experience as the sensation of green you might experience as the sensation I would call red, or what I feel as an ache you might feel as what I would call a tickle. Worse still, the functional meaning of the experience might be different. Suppose, for example, that when *I* feel pain I do my best to stop it, but that when *you* feel pain you want more of it. In that case my model would be useless.

But that, as we know, is actually extraordinarily unlikely. For the fact is — and it is a biological fact, and philosophers ought sometimes to pay more attention than they do to biology — that human beings are all members of the same biological species: all descended within recent history from common stock, all still sharing more than 999 thousandths of their genes in common, and all with brains which — at birth at least — could be interchanged without anyone being much the wiser. It is no more likely that two people will differ radically in the way their minds work than that two houses designed by the same architect to fill the same niche will differ in their structural principles. In fact, in one way it is even less likely. For houses themselves have no personal interest in architectural design, while human beings do have a personal interest in mind design. If, by some accident of evolution, I were to have a quite different kind of mind to you and every other human being, it would be my loss: because I would be a born failure at understanding others.

Of course, we should always expect that there will be certain differences. Every individual, as George Eliot commented in *Middlemarch*, has an 'equivalent centre of self, whence the light and shadows must always fall with a certain difference'. We can never count on one person being exactly like another – inside or out. But neither for that matter can we count on one house being exactly like another. The wallpaper in the house over the square may well be different to the wallpaper in mine. It could even be that I am wrong in thinking that the house has 'stairs' – it might have some cunning kind of hoist! But I have to say that with regard to the general structure of other people's houses I have, in the real world, seldom been caught out. Equally we are seldom caught out with other people's minds. There are 'crazy houses' – I've seen them in films: houses where the front door leads straight out the back, or a light switch sounds a fire alarm. There are 'crazy people', too – I have also seen *them* in films: a florid schizophrenic, say, whose feelings bear no relation to his actions, or a psychopath who is incapable of feeling guilt. But those are not the houses or the people we live among.

The truth is – and let me stress again that it is a biological truth rather than a strictly logical one – that for the most part we should expect our fellow human beings to have brains and minds very much like the one which each of us has as his personal exemplar. So much so that this trick of using

I understand you because we're BOTH human beings..
Why do WOMEN always want to UNDERSTAND chaps.?

oneself as a model for others serves – and always has served – human beings extremely well: better indeed than any other way of doing psychology known either to common sense or science.

In evolutionary terms it must have been a major breakthrough. Imagine the biological benefits to the first of our ancestors that developed the ability to make realistic guesses about the inner life of his rivals: to be able to picture what another was thinking about, and planning to do next, to be able to read the minds of others by reading his own. The way was open to a new deal in human social relationships: sympathy, compassion, trust, treachery and double-crossing – the very things which make us human.

But that way of telling it, is, as someone said, to put Descartes before the horse. Human beings are not the only social animals on earth. Couldn't this story of the inner eye and consciousness apply just as well to animals other than man?

FIVE

Is There Anybody There?

In his parable *Penguin Island* Anatole France relates how the old blind monk St Mael inadvertently baptized a group of penguins, mistaking them for men. When the news reached heaven it caused, so we are told, neither joy nor sorrow but an extreme surprise. The Lord himself was embarrassed. He gathered an assembly of clerics and doctors, and asked them for an opinion on the delicate question of whether the birds must now be given souls. It was a matter of more than theoretical importance. 'The Christian state', St Cornelius observed, 'is not without serious inconveniences for a penguin... The habits of birds are, in many points, contrary to the commandments of the Church.'[1] After lengthy discussion the learned fathers settled on a compromise. The baptized penguins were indeed to be granted souls – but, on St Catherine's recommendation, their souls were to be of small size.

The souls of penguins are not the most pressing issue raised by the two previous chapters. Yet in trying to assess the possibility that other animals are conscious, we must guard against what might be called 'St Catherine's error': the error of supposing that the capacity for consciousness must come in many different sizes, that it is something which is and always has been distributed to a greater or lesser degree throughout the animal kingdom; or that all animals – certainly all those with complex brains – are at least a little bit conscious. The fact is that consciousness – by which I mean no more nor less than the capacity to look in on the feelings, hopes, fears, etc. which correspond to the machinations of one's own brain – may exist in one size only: ours.

That is not to say that an inner eye, if and where it does exist in other species, would have to take exactly the same form as it does in human beings. External sense organs vary from species to species according to what their owners may require of them: higher visual acuity, for example, in one species, night vision in another, colour vision in another. By the same token, it is possible that the inner eye might also have a different 'conscious range' in different species, being tuned to different aspects of the brain's activity. None the less, logically and presumably physiologically, the self-reflective loop I sketched out on page 70 either exists as a loop or it does not. To me, at least, it makes no sense to suppose that before this loop evolved, animals were somehow partly conscious or even on their way to it. Water is not partly frozen at three degrees Celsius.

The question, then, is which species have crossed the conscious threshold, and which have not. We can approach an answer in two ways. Ideally we should look for direct evidence of conscious insight in individual animals. Failing that we can argue indirectly from their lifestyles. But the ideal studies have not yet been conducted – and no one knows quite how to do them.

I am going to play a kind of evolutionary game,

and the rule is this: if we have an idea of what something is for, and we can guess that a particular animal would have no use for it, we can be pretty sure that animal won't have it. If we know, for example, that wings are for flying, and we know enough about pigs to know that it would be no great advantage to a pig to fly, we could conclude – even if we did not know it already – that pigs do not have wings. The same goes for consciousness. If I am right in supposing that consciousness provides a basis for psychological understanding, and we can guess that a particular animal would have no great need of that, we have good reason to think that animal is not conscious.

By this criterion we must rule out most of the so-called lower animals. I do not think it would help an earthworm, a beetle or a frog to be conscious. Frogs, it is true, do sometimes interact with other frogs. But what would a frog lose if it was unable to imagine from the inside what it was like to be another frog? What would it lose if it was unable even to imagine what it was like to be itself? The answer must be not a lot – and not enough for there to be any biological need for a frog to have evolved an inner eye. How about the so-called social insects, such as honeybees? Certainly a beehive is an intricate community in which plenty of calculations must be made. But complex as it is, there is nothing psychologically complex about a beehive. Individual problems – conflicts of interest with other bees, and so on – simply do not arise there. The reason is that, in biological terms, the bees hardly have the status of individuals. Genetically the worker bees are so closely related to each other that they work together almost as one organism, putting the success of the whole hive before their own. Rivalry, jealousy, guilt and so on do not come in. There's nothing a bee would gain from being able to project its own feelings on to other bees.

We can skip the vast majority of other species: turtles, starlings, cows – all of whom, I think, could survive quite well without consciousness. For it is only when animals need to sustain lasting, intimate and difficult relationships with one another that conscious insight could begin to be of any real biological advantage: and that is only at the level of certain of the higher social mammals, a wolf-pack, say, a school of whales, a family of elephants or chimpanzees.

Yet even then I confess I am not sure. It would – I freely admit – be nice to think that wolves, elephants and tigers, for example, are cousins in consciousness to human beings. But their social arrangements are still primitive compared to those of the only animals we *know* are conscious, namely human beings themselves. From studies in the wild, chimpanzees alone stand out as animals which have reached a level of psychological involvement with their fellow animals such that consciousness might be essential.

Do chimpanzees speculate about the minds of other animals? I have said that there are no ideal experimental studies of insight in non-human species, but there is one study of one chimpanzee that bears directly on this question. David Premack did a clever experiment with a chimpanzee called Sarah, to see whether she had, as he put it, 'a theory of mind'.[2]

Premack showed Sarah videotapes of a human being in some sort of 'psychological' trouble: feeling cold; frustrated by not being able to escape from a locked cage; trying to get music from a gramophone which would not work. They were all situations which the chimpanzee – who had lived for a long time in a human environment – had experienced for herself. The question was, would Sarah realize, on the basis of her own reading of the situation, her own inner analysis of what was happening, how the human felt – and so know what to do?

Premack gave Sarah a set of photographs showing possible solutions to the human being's dilemma: a key to the cage, a connecting lead for the gramophone, etc., and he gave her the opportunity to match the photographs to each of the videotaped problems (a procedure with which, in a different context, she was already quite familiar). He reports that Sarah did indeed choose the right solution – but only if the individual in trouble was someone Sarah liked!

It suggests to Premack – and no one but an extreme sceptic could dispute it – that chimpanzees do have insight into the way their own minds work, and so can imagine from the inside what it is like to be in someone else's place. To anyone who has ever lived or worked with chimpanzees that surely comes as no surprise. I myself once shared a hut in Africa with a young chimpanzee (for four weeks only, although it seemed very much longer), and quickly came to realize that her mindreading skills were in several ways quite the equal of my own.

Yet I have to say that anyone who has ever lived with a domestic dog might be tempted to draw an exactly similar conclusion. I have lived with my dog for fourteen years, and sometimes I do not doubt that he is conscious. But *is* he? If dogs are conscious, the evidence I would finally require is that the dog himself can, like a chimpanzee, put his consciousness to use. I sometimes project my feelings on to him. Does he – if he has any – project his on to me? Can he guess from his own experience what I am feeling? If, for example, he sees me shivering, does he understand I am cold? When I prick my finger, does he find himself imagining how he would feel if he were me?

I find myself thinking so in general, and yet almost never in particular. Last night my dog watched me in the bath. He himself has had a bath. He could in principle use his own experience as a model for understanding mine. Yet nothing in the way he watched me convinces me of that. When *he* has been bathed he has always looked to me as though he finds the experience mildly insulting and uncomfortable, but nothing suggests he thought that *I* might be feeling insulted or uncomfortable, or indeed that he thought I was feeling anything at all.

The study of Sarah is the only experiment I know which bears directly on this issue, and no one has yet tried it with any other species than the chimpanzee. But there is a weaker test of consciousness which has been tried with a whole range of different animals. This is the 'mirror-test', devised by Gordon Gallupp to see whether animals have a sense of 'self'.

When an 18-month-old human infant is placed before a mirror, he or she will regularly show 'self-directed behaviour'. The child recognizes that the image in the mirror is an image of himself – and, for example, if he sees that the face in the mirror has a red spot on its forehead, he will start fingering the mark on his own head. How does a chimpanzee react if he is allowed to use a mirror to examine a spot on his own head? It turns out that, like the

child, the chimp does direct his attention to himself. So does an orang-utan. So, recent evidence suggests, does a beluga whale. But a dog *doesn't*, a baboon doesn't, a cat doesn't: these, and every other species tested, always treat the mirror-image as if it were the image of a stranger – and soon enough they stop reacting to it at all. It is not that a dog, or a baboon, is too stupid, or scatty, or uninterested in images, to connect the mirror-image with itself: it is that they seem quite unable to grasp the concept of self. The strong implication is that these animals have no way of reflecting on their own states of mind, that they never think '*I* want this, *I* feel that', and *a fortiori* that they could never imagine 'This is how *I* should feel if I were you'.

Descartes believed there were indeed no other conscious animals on earth. In that, we can justifiably conclude, he went too far. The great apes we can be fairly sure of, perhaps whales as well. Yet Descartes was as nearly right as makes no matter. If we walk down an English country lane, we walk by ourselves. Trees, birds, bees, the rabbit darting down its hole, the cow heavy with milk waiting at the farmer's gate are all as without insight into their condition as the dummies on show at Madame Tussaud's.

That, I think, is the reasonable conclusion. It cannot be an altogether welcome one. Let me say at once why I think it is not a conclusion which anyone should take too much to heart. 'You throw the sand against the wind', William Blake wrote, 'and the wind blows it back again.' The point is that it hardly matters how animals may or may not feel about themselves, when our business finally is with how *we* feel about them.

Suppose Descartes, or I, had argued that a

banana is not aware of its own colour, or a rose aware of its own scent, would it have any bearing on our perception of the banana as yellow or the rose as sweet? Not at all. Then why, when it is argued that a frog does not itself feel pain, or a blackbird feel proud of its song, should it have any bearing on whether *we* see the frog as suffering or the bird as feeling proud?

Henry More's accusation against Descartes was that he 'snatched away life and sensibility from all the animals'. But More seems not to have realized that in the end only More himself could – if he chose – snatch away such sensibilility because *he himself put it there in the first place.* Consciousness, as they say, is in the eye of the beholder.

Kant, in the *Critique of Judgement*, wrote about beauty, but he might have been writing about consciousness:

> Whenever we estimate beauty we do not seek any criterion from experience, but judge for ourselves aesthetically whether the thing is beautiful... Such an estimation does not depend on what nature is, but on how we look at it. If nature had produced its forms for our satisfaction ... it would be a grace done to us by nature, whereas in fact we confer one upon her.[3]

And, in the same spirit, A. N. Whitehead:

> Nature gets credit which should in truth be reserved for ourselves: the rose for its scent; the nightingale for his song; the sun for his radiance... The poets are entirely mistaken. They should address their lyrics to themselves, and should turn them into odes of self-congratulation on the excellency of the

human mind. Nature is a dull affair, soundless, scentless, colourless; merely the hurrying of material, endlessly, meaninglessly.[4]

The mystic, the poet, or any ordinary person who animates nature by the power of his own mind – who sees faces in the clouds, hears whispers on the wind, and feels himself in sympathy with every living thing is *not in error*. Far from it: for nothing which helps us to relate to and interpret our environment *can* be an error.

Remember this: the only consciousness we know of directly is our own. When we see consciousness even in another human being, we are seeing only what we ourselves project. No one gives us permission – philosophical or scientific – to do it. But from childhood on we learn to do it, because in practice it works wonders for our understanding of how other *people* think and act. If, in practice, it works wonders for our understanding of the non-human world as well, so much the better.

Does it work for the non-human world? The American zoologist, H. S. Jennings, wrote in 1906:

> We do not usually attribute consciousness to a stone, because this would not assist us in understanding or controlling the behaviour of the stone. Practically indeed it would lead us much astray in dealing with such an object. On the other hand, we usually do attribute consciousness to the dog, because this is useful; it enables us practically to appreciate, foresee, and control its actions much more readily than we could otherwise do so... An amoeba is a beast of prey. If an amoeba ... were as large as a whale, it is quite conceivable that occasions might arise when the attribution to it of

elemental states of consciousness might save the un-sophisticated human being from the destruction that would result from the lack of such attribution.[5]

Jennings came as close as anyone to seeing that human consciousness may have a value to us far beyond its original – I would say its evolutionary – domain in the area of interpersonal psychology. But maybe still he underestimated the practical uses of attributing consciousness even to a stone. A child who thinks two magnets *like* each other, a gardener who thinks his plants *want* watering, a Christian who believes that God has *forgiven* him his sins, are on to a way of looking at inanimate nature which is by no means to be disparaged. Indeed a conscious model of the universe, based on our own reading of ourselves, may well be the most powerful general theory that there is.

I began a few pages back to take away consciousness where objectively, scientifically and philosophically I think it cannot belong. The glory of human beings is that they will put it back. The inner eye may have evolved for one purpose and one purpose only – to enable people to read the behaviour of other people like themselves – but with it we have the capacity to make *our minds* the measure of all things.

SIX
Sentimental Education

There is a painting by Ilya Repin that hangs in the Tretyakov Gallery in Moscow, its title *They did not expect him*. The artist has expressed himself in two dimensions, but we see his work almost immediately in five: three of space, one of time, and one of human consciousness. In slow motion, this is how I interpret the human content of the scene.

A man – still in his coat, dirty boots – enters a drawing room. The maid is apprehensive. She could close the door; but she does not – she wants to see how he is received. The grandmother stands, alarmed, as though she has seen a ghost. The younger woman – eyes wide – registers delighted disbelief. The girl – taking her cue from the grown-ups – is suddenly shy. Only the boy shows open pleasure.

Who is he? Perhaps the father of the family. His children, his wife, his own mother. They thought he had been taken away. And now he has walked in, as if from the dead. His mother cannot believe it; his wife did not dare hope; the son was secretly confident that he would return.

Where's he been? The maid's face shows a degree of disapproval; the son's excited pride. The man's eyes, tired and staring, tell of a nightmare from which he himself is only beginning to emerge.

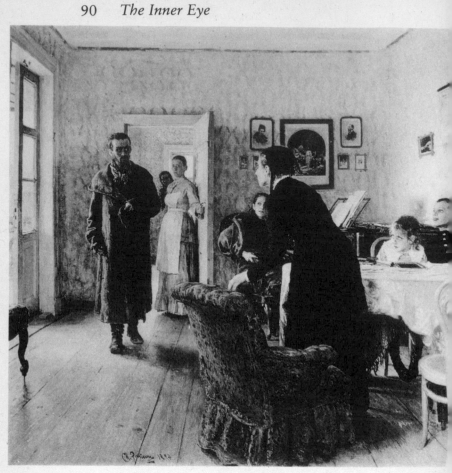

Ilya Repin, *They did not expect him*, 1884,
Tretyakov Gallery, Moscow

The painting represents, as it happens, a Russian political prisoner, who has been released from the Tsar's gaols and come back home. More information may be needed for you or I to catch the final nuance. But try interpreting a scene like this without reference to consciousness, to what *we* know of human feelings, and the depth, its human depth, completely disappears.

I give this example to illustrate how clever we all are. Apprehension, disbelief, disapproval, weariness, etc. are concepts of such subtlety that I doubt if any of us could explain in words just what they mean. Yet in dissecting this scene – or any other human situation – we wield these concepts with remarkable authority, operating almost like a master surgeon who knows exactly the instrument that he requires, and can rely on it coming immediately to hand. '*Nurse!* . . . scalpel, forceps, needle!'. '*Self!* . . . hope, pride, fear . . .'

But it was not always so. There was – of course – a time in all our lives when we ourselves had experienced none of the relevant emotions, and therefore had none of these conceptual instruments to work with. By what age you or I might first have been able to make sense of Repin's picture I do not know. But I know that something very interesting had to happen to us first: we each had to begin the long and difficult apprenticeship of learning *for ourselves* what it feels like *from the inside* to be a human being.

Although such learning continues throughout life, the first few years are crucial. A newborn child still has it all to learn. He has yet to establish that he himself exists. He has no history whatever of personal experience. His own feelings when they first occur to him belong to no one, and explain nothing. He still has to discover what it means to have a mind, let alone that other human beings have minds like his. Yet within two years, this same child will already be capable of projecting his own mind on to other people – recognizing, or at least guessing at, their thoughts and feelings.

Indeed, almost as soon as a child can talk, he talks the language of natural psychology, using and understanding words like 'I', 'think', 'want', 'happy', 'sad' and so on. 'We have evidence', write two researchers who studied the conversation between young children and their mothers, 'that 28-month-old children interpret their own and other people's mental states, comment on their own or someone else's expected and past experiences, and discuss how their own or someone else's state might be changed or what gave rise to it.'[1] Although the evidence for it is utterances of the sort 'You sad Mummy. What Daddy do?', 'Grandma mad, 'cos I wrote on wall', these 2-year-old children are clearly well on their way to acquiring the skills that you and I used with Repin's picture. Even younger children, before they can speak, may demonstrate by deed if not by word that they are in touch with another person's inner world. A child of 18 months may offer his own comfort blanket to mother when he detects that she is upset, another may deliberately steal his sister's comfort blanket *in order* to upset her. The actions may be fumbling, but the analysis that lies behind them is impressively correct.

The significance of this transition from a newborn baby's state of existential ignorance to that of a self-reflective, other-oriented 2-year-old, hardly needs emphasizing. It is the focus of the best work in child psychology, and since so much has been written about it, there is nothing I can say here that is more than by the way. But let us consider what looks like a relatively straightforward question. What, for example, are the minimum requirements for a child to attribute to someone else the elementary mental state of feeling 'sad'? Logically, it would seem that at least three stages must be passed. (*1*) The child has himself to have *been* sad, i.e. to have had something sad-making happen to him, and to have responded to it in a human way; (*2*) he has to have been *aware* that he is sad, i.e. to have noticed his own mental state and related it to his own behaviour; and (*3*) he has to have discovered that what he feels might in principle be felt by someone else.

The first of these three stages is, of course, reached quickly, and it might be thought that in reaching that stage a child necessarily reaches the second stage as well. No baby lives beyond a week without apparently – behaviourally and physiologically, that is – being upset by one or other of life's inevitable insults. Indeed, babies seem to find a good deal of life upsetting. Who doubts then that a sad-looking baby, a sad-sounding baby is also a baby who is *aware* of feeling sad?

I have to say that I do. As we saw in previous chapters, the fact that a child is *in* a particular state is no guarantee that he is *consciously aware* of it. My dog, too, may behave as if he is feeling sad – when I go out and leave him, say, or when he is not allowed another piece of cake – but I am fairly sure that he is not aware of the emotion. For the very same reasons that we should doubt the existence of consciousness in animals, we should, I think, doubt the existence of consciousness in human babies for at least the first few months of life. It may, of course, suit us as adults to believe that when a 3-month-old baby smiles he is consciously feeling pleasure, or to worry that when he cries he's feeling pain – and that indeed is our prerogative. 'It is the physical weakness of a baby that makes it seem innocent, not the quality of its inner life', wrote St Augustine. 'I myself have seen a baby jealous; it was too young to speak, but it was livid with anger as it watched another baby at the breast.'[2] But it is precisely the quality of its inner life that is in doubt. So far as the baby in his own right is concerned, there is no evidence that he has an inner life at all.

At what point a human child does first become capable of 'looking in' on his own mental states – when exactly the inner eye becomes connected – no one knows. Certainly it takes at least a year before children pass either of the tests that I mentioned previously as being applied to animals. No child less than a year old can recognize himself in a mirror (and many not till 18 months or more). Nor, before that, do children show any other outward signs that they have any sort of *theory* of what it is like to be a human being.

Still, it must come, and it does – probably some time early in the second year. From that point on the child begins to be aware of his own thoughts and feelings, and he can start to develop a model of how his own mind works. Yet the remarkable thing is that he doesn't just apply this self-model to himself: almost immediately he starts using it to make sense of other people too, attributing to them with a fair degree of accuracy the very states of mind which he has just discovered beneath the surface of his own behaviour.

The problems are considerable. How, for a start,

I'm not letting on all I understand until I find out what the ADULTS want from me..

does the child choose from his own accumulating library of inner experience the *right* concept to make sense of someone else – how does he make better than random connections between all the different things that he felt yesterday and the particular thing the other person may be feeling now? He sees his mother looking glum. Does he think to himself 'I wonder whether she's feeling (*a*) sad, (*b*) happy, (*c*) hot, (*d*) hungry – let me try each of those different hypotheses and see'?

That would, to say the least, be asking a great deal of him. You and I, sophisticated adults that we are, may be able to home in on the appropriate explanation right away. But for the 2-year-old, just beginning, some kind of teaching-aid is surely needed, something which helps him to look up and lock into the relevant experience without doing too much searching. If there is such an aid, it is provided, I suspect, by the phenomenon of 'empathy'.

Empathy means feeling simultaneously with others: not just imagining at one remove another person's state of mind but experiencing that very feeling in one's own person right now – seeing someone else in distress and having tears come to one's own eyes; hearing their laughter and finding oneself smiling with them. All of us still sometimes find it happening to us, but it is in early childhood that such empathic responses are most obvious and pronounced. The other day I saw a 2-year-old girl observe her older sister come running in from the garden looking thoroughly miserable; the little girl's own face puckered and in a moment she herself was wailing.

We might, of course, dismiss such an episode as no more than childish confusion about who was feeling sad. I suspect there is more to it than that.

The little girl was a mere beginner in the art of doing psychology. But even as a beginner it would have been natural to her to be looking for some sort of inner explanation for how her sister was behaving — some reference point within herself. Perhaps she initially had several possibilities to play with, and yet no immediate way of matching any particular one of her own feelings to her sister's, until, that is, she found tears welling up in *her own* eyes — and the mental state she needed to explain her sister was literally before her inner eye.

How does it happen that emotional states are catching in this way? If empathy is to do the job that I am suggesting — namely to introduce the child to a state of mind that he is still unsure of — the answer can hardly be that the child has first to recognize the feeling and then reproduce it, for in that case nothing would have been gained. It must presumably work more directly. Let's take the girl again. Her sister came in looking miserable; the 2-year-old observed her; her own face changed; she began to look miserable, and then began to cry. Could it be that by the simple act of *imitating her sister's facial expression* she was directly creating the corresponding feelings in herself?

Common wisdom has it so: smile and you'll feel happy, knit your brows and you'll feel stern. But this idea has now gone some way beyond folklore. There is recent scientific evidence to show that making the right face does in fact produce the appropriate emotion. When an actor for example 'tries on a face', not only may he report that his mood changes with it — from anger, say, to happiness, to grief — but physiological measures show that there are changes in his autonomic nervous system, producing subtle shifts in the blood flow through his limbs and brain, exactly as would happen if the mood were 'genuine'.

This would not have been news to certain earlier writers in this area. Montaigne claimed that he himself could fall ill simply by looking at another person who was sick. Nietzsche believed that 'physiognomic' imitation plays a crucial role throughout our lives.

> To understand another person, that is *to imitate his feelings in ourselves*, we ... produce the feeling after the *effects* it exerts and displays on the other person by imitating with our own body the expression of his eyes, his voice, his bearing. Then a similar feeling arises in us in consequence of an ancient association. We have brought our skill in understanding the feelings of others to a high state of perfection and in the presence of another person we are always almost involuntarily practising this skill.[3]

But that is to exaggerate the role it plays. In looking at Repin's painting, for example, I do not, as a matter of fact, find myself responding empathically – actually feeling the apprehension, surprise, etc. for myself – let alone do I imitate all the various different faces. But that perhaps is because I, like you, no longer need to. After years of practice, we can call up the relevant concepts without having to go through the imitative motions Nietzsche talks of. None the less, for children as distinct from adults, empathy may be an essential trick for helping psychological understanding to get under way: a walking frame to help the child with its first steps in understanding – but a crutch which as adults we no longer need.

That is perhaps how it gets going. But for a small child, the journey has only just begun. In trying to analyse the world of others around him, a 2-year-old is bound to find that his everyday experiences, however well internally observed, however accurately attributed to other people, will get him only so far. What he needs now is to extend his own experiential range: to have more experiences to feel and reflect on in himself, a wider knowledge of the possibilities of human feeling, sharper instruments for analysing other people.

'You *sad* Mummy. What Daddy do?' Well actually – if the child could only recognize it – it is not exactly sadness that his mother is feeling: it is depression, gloom, grief, frustration, or whatever – varieties of sadness the child does not yet know anything about. 'What Daddy do?' Well, little one, the fact is that Daddy's drunk again, Daddy's having supper with another woman, Daddy's lost his job. Or perhaps it is that Mummy *always* feels like this during her period, or when she thinks about the atom bomb. Needless to say, those answers would be lost on the small child.

It is a daunting journey that still lies ahead of him. So many things still to learn – and all to be learned and internalized through *personal* experience. The question is, what drives him on? What biological imperatives, if any, lie behind the child's search for experience? The ability to do psychology is, as we saw, a biologically adaptive trait in human beings. Can it be that nature has provided human beings with only half the answer: that she has, as it were, given every child a key to the library of the human mind, given him eyes to read, but then left it entirely up to him to stock his own library shelves?

Let us look again at what the problem is – and

presumably always has been – for any ordinary human being. A child is born with no history whatever of personal experience. The rooms are blank, the library shelves are empty. But within a few years that child must – if he is to be any good at all as a psychologist – have filled his head with a vast range of inner knowledge about what it is like to be a 'typical' human being.

The child can, it is true, count on a good deal of that knowledge coming to him by accident, simply as a result of his being a living, growing, accident-prone child. No one is going to escape, for example, the basic experiences of being hungry, hurt, happy, lonely, and so on. But there are still whole ranges of experience which the child cannot count on happening by accident, and which may none the less be of crucial importance to his understanding of, and ability to cope with, other people. What chance that, even in time, he will learn what it is like to have his own child die, or to be cheated by a trusted friend, or to engage in an adulterous love-affair? Yet such experiences are the very stuff of human social living.

True, a particular individual may get away with it – get away, that is, with being ignorant of the 'inner meaning' of large areas of other people's lives. But in the long course of human evolution, it must surely have been those who from earliest youth amassed the widest range of personal experience who were best prepared to meet whatever social situations came their way. In fact, if psychology means survival, and experience means psychology, then experience means survival. Since we ourselves are the descendants of none other than those who did survive, shouldn't we find that every member of the human species is predisposed from birth to internalize all the experiences he can? There do exist, I believe, natural – 'instinctive' – strategies for extending personal experience which effectively ensure that even the most unenterprising human being living the most sheltered life is rapidly introduced to a surprisingly rich and representative sample of the possibilities of human feeling.

The start of it lies in the long, long period that children have in which to develop towards psychological maturity. Human childhood is a remarkable biological invention. All animals have to grow up, of course, but in very few animals is growing up as delayed as it is in human beings. There is no animal which exploits childhood quite as human beings do – as a period for social and *emotional* development.

Let's say that children do not become independent – socially or biologically – until the age of about fifteen years. That is fifteen years of preparation and practice for adult life, in a protective environment where – however it seems to the child – nothing much has to be taken all that seriously; years of watching, investigating, seeing what may happen. If it doesn't snow this winter, perhaps it will next. If you don't catch measles this year, perhaps you will next. A child will have eaten 10,000 meals before he ever has to provide food for himself. But much more important he will have been in tens of fights, experienced hundreds of bouts of tears and consolation, been the hero of a dozen birthday parties before he ever comes to the fights or the tears or the celebrations which really matter – where his own social or even biological survival is at issue.

During all that time the child is, as it were, playing with Monopoly money, and with nature's help he will 'Pass Go' on every round. But that, to repeat, is not how it appears to him at the moment of the game. A little girl's hair will grow in a few months; but when, as George Eliot in *The Mill on the Floss* describes happening to Maggie, her brother chops it off for her, the emotion is as keen and as significant as any she will ever feel again.

> She sat as helpless and despairing among her black locks as Ajax among the slaughtered sheep. Very trivial, perhaps, this anguish seems to weather-worn mortals who have to think of Christmas bills, dead loves and broken friendships, but it was not less bitter to Maggie... Every one of such keen moments has left its trace and lives in us still, but such traces have blent themselves irrevocably with the firmer texture of our youth and manhood; and so it comes that we can look on at the troubles of our children with a smiling disbelief in the reality of their pain... Surely, if we could recall that early bitterness, and the dim guesses, the strangely per-spectiveless conception of life that gave our bitter-ness its intensity, we should not pooh-pooh the griefs of our children.[4]

No, nor should we pooh-pooh their moments of de-light and madcap joy.

I am bound, of course, to draw upon my own ex-perience as a source of ideas about what childhood is about, so let me say something about the way that I grew up. I do not for a moment suppose my life was wholly typical. But it was typical enough in its childishness and its intensity.

My family was a large one – at home there were seldom less than ten at any meal, and on holidays generally more. I had four brothers and sisters, and seventeen first cousins. We went round in droves, stayed in each other's houses and met up regularly at my grandmother's Sunday teaparties. We were a scientific lot. On one notable occasion my grandmother bought a sheep's head from the butcher, and we dissected it on the kitchen table after tea. My grandfather held up the lenses of the eyes for us to look through: a beautifully clear image, and everything turned upside down. We were encouraged to be active *experimenters* – nothing (except our own family existence) to be taken for granted. The way to find out about things was to try them for, or on, yourself. My father, a doctor, would regularly use his own blood – or ours – for his research. He once (by mistake, I think) managed to make his trousers radioactive. Secretly I took it as a model of scientific method. Self-experiment became the rule. At school we stole chloroform from the science-room and gassed ourselves silly. I shot a starling with an air-rifle, and challenged God to strike me down. At the age of ten I had to pray every Sunday that 'from fornication and all other deadly sins, good Lord deliver us' – and so I and my friends experimented, none too successfully, with fornication too.

The grown-ups were there to test us, tease us, and inform us. We admired and imitated them. One was a communist, one a Conservative MP, one had a Nobel prize, one (or two) were homosexual, one was in trouble with the police, one was a hundred years old, a favourite aunt had *three* abortions... We knew all that. Not always because we were told, but because we made it our business to find out – and listen in.

By the time I reached adulthood myself, there were not many areas of human feeling I had not at least tried on for size. Sometimes it was calculated. After I left school I worked for a while in Plymouth and lived off five shillings a week to see what it felt like to be poor. It meant I ended up sleeping in the pyjamas of my landlady's dead husband – which she sold me for a shilling! But as often as not these experiments in living just happened – as they happen, I think, to most normal human children. And the way they mostly happen is through *play*.

What is play? Perhaps it is easiest to say first what it is not. It is not living off five shillings a week, when five shillings is all you have. It is not being really in trouble with the police. If there is one element common to all kinds of play – from rough-and-tumble in the playground, to the most intense and secret fantasy-games behind the hen-house – it is surely this: play is a way of experimenting with possible feelings and possible identities

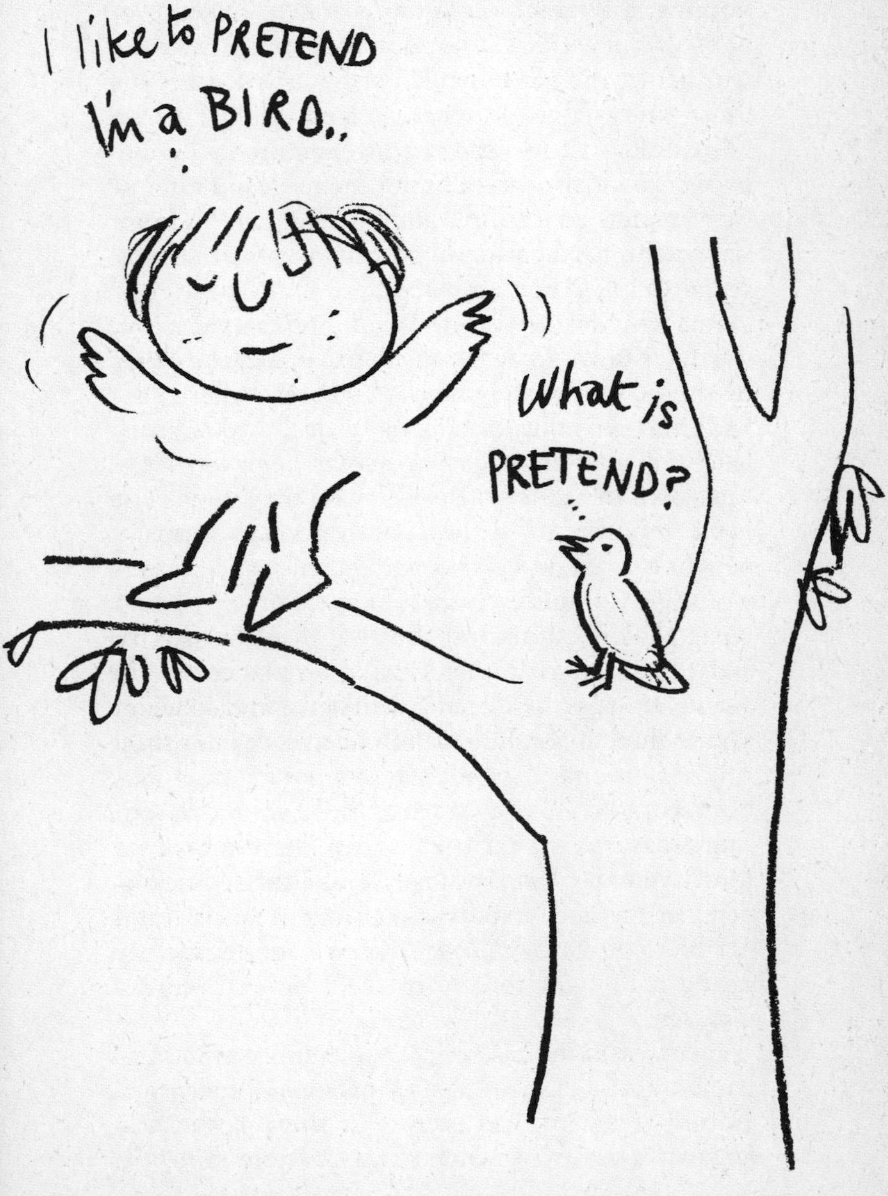
I like to PRETEND
I'm a BIRD..
What is
PRETEND?

without risking the real biological or social consequences. Cut! Time for tea, time to go home – and nothing in the real world has changed, except perhaps that *the child* is not quite the person that he was before, he has extended just a little further his inner knowledge of what it can feel like to be human. Play is the way by which children – largely by their own efforts – gain for themselves a kind of 'sentimental education', and nothing can be more important to their development as sensitive and socially-skilled human beings.

But why do they do it? What motivates them at the time? It would be too much to ask of a child that he should deliberately go out and seek experiences with his own education as the goal. But this problem – the problem of getting human beings to act in their own interests when otherwise they might not want or bother to – is not, in evolutionary terms, a new one. It could be said with equal justice that it would be too much to ask of any ordinary human being that he should deliberately feed himself in order to sustain the biochemical balance of his blood, or that he should deliberately indulge in sexual intercourse in order to procreate his genes. The evolutionary solution in the latter cases has been to make the relevant activities a source of sensual pleasure: we eat because we like the taste of food, we make love because we like the sensations of intimacy and sexual orgasm – and so we fulfil our biological 'obligations' without our necessarily giving a thought to any of the long-term consequences.

Likewise in the case of the 'obligation' to gain as wide a spread as possible of personal experience. Natural selection has seen to it that, in the first instance anyway, we do it simply because it is *fun*:

the pursuit of novel experience, and especially novel kinds of social interaction, is one of the chief pleasures for a growing child, and children in play will try out almost everything that's going, exploring the limits of their bodies and their minds – simply because they are there.

Generally it is children themselves who take the initiative in play: they do so because it gives them pleasure. But since the child carries the biological hopes of his parents and relations – since if the child fails, the parents ultimately fail – it makes biological sense that parents also should take an active part in the child's quest for experience. And indeed, with younger children anyway, it is the parents who – in the interests of their child, but also because it gives *them* pleasure – not only play an important role as partners in the games but provide the dolls, pay for the rides, organize the parties and so on. It is the parents, too, who (in more than half the families in Britain) will introduce a pet animal into the family. Like a mother cat who brings home a live mouse for her kittens to 'play' with, so Daddy buys a dog for the child to exercise his love, anxiety and spite on.

Yet the involvement of parents and other adults may have a darker side, indeed it may be crucial that it does so. For wide as its scope may be, play, as a means of psychological self-education, has important limitations. Most obviously there are some things that children *in pursuit of pleasure* simply will not get around to – that in fact, they will actively avoid. A child in play is not, if he can help it, going to suffer unjust treatment, he is not going knowingly to bring down punishment on his own head, he is not going to court the hostility of friends and loved ones. It may happen by chance or accident, but it may not; and if it does not, the child himself may be the loser. To the extent that his own future success with other people depends on his having a complete picture of the possibilities of human feeling, it is essential that he should have personal experience not only of the pleasures but also the miseries that can and do affect his fellow human beings.

The problem is potentially quite serious. If a solution has been found, the answer I see has been that adults should come in with the 'hard sell'. If children will not learn, there are, it seems, those ready and willing to teach them. Both as individuals and as a society, we, as adults, are in fact remarkably manipulative of children – and manipulative in patently harsh ways. Some of it may of course be unavoidable, as when a mother at her own wits' end leaves a child to cry, or innocently makes a child jealous by tending to his sibling. But more surprising – and more interesting – are those cases where the child's distress *is* avoidable, but where the parents, far from helping to reduce it, exacerbate the situation, sometimes apparently playing a calculated game. Robert Southey records as one of his earliest childhood memories:

> My feelings were very acute; they used to amuse themselves by making me cry at sad songs and dismal stories ... [until] I used to beg them not to proceed.[5]

By the standards of the past, that is comparatively mild. Lloyd deMause, in 'The evolution of childhood', describes how, since time immemorial, children have been systematically put on the rack by the very adults who had them in their care. For example:

The number of ghost-like figures used to frighten children throughout history is legion, and their regular use by adults was common until quite recently... For instance, in Germany until recently ... during the first week in December, adults would dress up in terrifying costumes and pretend to be a messenger of Christ who would punish children and tell them if they would get Christmas presents or not.[6]

it's all about GROWN-UP feelings..

Some GROWN-UPS Seem awfully CHILDISH to me..

Some of the games which deMause describes as 'typical of adult–child interaction in the past' were more elaborate still. Jean-Paul Richter went to the trouble of hiring men to dress up as brigands armed with swords and pistols, who were instructed to set upon him and his 9-year-old son while they were out for a walk in the woods – so that his son should learn the meaning of fear through this 'sportive representation of alarming circumstances'.

Such practices – 'jokes', 'teases', 'initiations', 'rites of passage' – are so widely recorded, and from so many cultures other than our own, that I do not think we can (as deMause himself would like to do) simply dismiss them as a pathological perversion of the tender relationship which ought to exist between parents and their offspring. Children need stretching, and they cannot or will not always do it for themselves.

I am not, as it happens, able to draw on my own experience here, for so far as I remember my own family gave me a comparatively easy time. Does that mean there are areas of human experience I missed out on? Perhaps yes ... but perhaps no. As a matter of fact I *was* set on by brigands several times before I was 10 years old. And it was not only to me that such things happened. Here is a 7-year-old boy relating what happened to *him* one night:

> I was captured by cannibals. They all began to jump and yell. I was surprised to see myself in my own parlour. There was a fire and a kettle was over it full of boiling water. They threw me into it and once in a while the cook used to come over and stick a fork in me to see if I was cooked.[7]

Despite what was said above about the improbability that a child left to himself will contrive to extend his own experience into such unknown and dangerous areas, it can sometimes happen – and the place it happens is in *dreams*.

SEVEN

A Book at Bedtime?

A letter appeared in the *Listener* magazine a few years ago:

> Sir: A footnote to the 'Making of Mankind' tv series. In dreams involving flight from a menace, I always find myself running chimp fashion, with knuckles on the ground... So now I know *what it feels like* to move quadrupedally.[1]

If people can discover in dreams what it feels like to be another kind of animal, then might they not discover – to much greater effect – what it feels like to be another kind of human being? Kate Phillips, a young midwife, clearly thought so:

> I think most midwives dream about giving birth when they start working in maternity units, and it was a fairly common experience among the students that I trained with ... I've never myself been pregnant. But my dreams have certainly made me more understanding, more relaxed and more confident in talking to mothers.[2]

But first, what are some of the facts about human dreaming? While we sleep, our bodies are shut down and our senses become dead to outside stimulation. But four or five times a night our brains enter a stage known as active sleep. Recordings from the scalp show that the brain itself appears to have woken up. These periods are marked by the occurrence of rapid eye movements (REM) – the eyeballs darting around beneath the lids. It is during these periods of REM sleep that some people will, if they are woken, most likely report that they have been dreaming.

It used to be thought that there was a simple relationship between REM and dreaming. But people do dream at other times of the sleep-cycle, and even during REM they are not always dreaming. For the first few years of life the presence of REM may indeed have no particular significance. Babies and infants actually spend more time in REM sleep than older children do; but when a 3-year-old is woken up during REM sleep he will have very little to report – no more than a simple bodily sensation or a thought going round his head. It is not until the age of five or so, that the first evidence appears of full-fledged imaginative dreams. But from then on dreaming becomes the dominant feature of our sleeping lives. Once we are 'grown-up' enough to dream, we dream about one and half hours a night – night after night, year after year.

Many animals show a similar pattern of brain activity and eye movements during sleep, and it has been widely assumed that they, too, are dreaming. Given, however, that REM, even in human beings, has no necessary link to dreaming, the inference is probably not justified. Certainly it seems unlikely that animals' dreams, if they occur at all, are anything like ours. An animal such as a dog, which when it is awake falls far short of a 3-year-old

ARE DREAMS REAL?
Where do DREAMS come from? Why tell them?
If I INVENT a DREAM will he know? And does it matter?
Even a poor DREAM is better than NONE at all?
He DREAMS- therefore he EXISTS...

human child in terms of its capacity for self-awareness and inventiveness, is hardly likely to exceed it when it is asleep.

Everything suggests that we human beings have taken advantage of this phase of sleep to do something that is biologically unique, something very special on an experiential level, which no other animal does or needs to do. There have, of course, been many theories about what that something is. Yet few theorists have looked for a biologically adaptive function, and only one – David Foulkes[3] – has come close to seeking such a function in *the need for a natural psychologist to extend to the limit his personal experience of being a human being.*

Let us go to one of the most perfectly observed descriptions of childhood (and pay no attention to the fact that it was written by Charles Darwin's granddaughter, for there is no reason to think that Gwen Raverat (née Darwin) was unduly influenced by her grandfather's ideas). In *Period Piece* she writes:

My room was always full of dreams. The worst one was of Joan of Arc. She came one windy night in full armour, and galloped up and down the passage outside my bedroom, stopping sometimes to shake and bang at my door and vow that she would kill me when she got in.

I often dreamt I was a horse, and I know exactly what it feels like to be one. I even know what it feels like to be able to twitch the skin on my shoulder, and shudder away a fly. Once I dreamt that I was a young yellow mare, and I was trying to hide behind a gorse bush from a very wicked bull.

I was generally a boy, swimming rivers with a

dagger in my mouth, or riding for my life with a
message, or shooting my way out of a fray; in fact, I
led at night a sort of Henty existence of most pleas-
urably exciting adventures.[4]

What strikes me here is that this little girl who discovered through her dreams 'exactly what it felt
like' to be a horse, was almost certainly discovering
in her other night-time adventures a thousand other
feelings of much more obvious and immediate relevance to human social life.

If waking play can do it, why not dreams?
Dreams, like play, would seem to allow the child to
experiment with his or her own feelings, without
suffering the consequences the dream events would
have in the real world. Could not dreams be yet
another naturally evolved technique – perhaps the
most ingenious natural teaching aid there is – for
helping human beings to do psychology?

I have asked people directly: 'Do you think that
in a dream you *could* experience feelings you have
never felt before, and so perhaps discover for the
first time what those feelings might be like for
someone else?' And there seems at first to be an
obvious objection. Since dreams are bound to be
based largely on memories of things we have
already experienced in waking life, there would
seem to be no way that a dream could ever teach us
anything really 'new' about ourselves. If the dream
is to give *new* insight, it can only work by putting
the dreamer into an imaginary situation never
before experienced. If a person has never been in a
situation before, how can he possibly *imagine* it?
No one can pull himself up by his own bootstraps –
and yet isn't that precisely what I am suggesting has
to happen?

True enough there must be limits to imagination. A Kalahari Bushman who has never come across snow in waking life could not, I suppose, invent snow in a dream; and the same goes for numerous other elementary experiences, where our subjective response is determined primarily by the objective nature of the environmental stimulus. The taste of cheese, the sound of thunder, the look of the Eiffel Tower – no one could invent those in a dream. But for a great range of human experiences, including almost all the socially important ones, our feelings do not depend so much on the objective nature of a stimulus as on what, subjectively, we make of it, and that will be determined by what we take to be its context.

Thus my response, for example, to hearing a gun go off depends on whether I am – or at least believe myself to be – on a grouse moor, at a fairground, or walking down an alley in New York. My response to seeing a pool of blood depends on whether it is – or at least I believe it to be – my own blood, my child's blood, or the blood of a carcase on the butcher's table. Change the context and you have changed the meaning.

Now, while it's clearly the case that if I have never heard a gun go off, I shall not be able to imagine it, and if I have never been to New York I shall not be able to imagine that either, it is not necessarily true that if *I have never heard a gun go off in New York* I shall not be able to imagine *that*. Because all I may have to do to set up this unprecedented situation is to take two familiar events and combine them in a novel way. Thus fantasy can in principle be a creative process. In fact, it can work rather like a language. Certainly, no one can *say* anything at all unless he has an elementary vocabulary, but granted he has that vocabulary he can, by recombining the elements in different – even random – ways, then say a thousand novel and surprising things.

So with dreams, images taken from waking experience at other times and other places can be recombined in ways that surprise even the 'dream-artist' who creates it. Consider, for example, another of Gwen Raverat's dream stories (so full of incident, that I have here shortened her account to half its length).

> Once I dreamt a regular ghost story. I thought that Mrs Phillips, our housekeeper, came to my father and said: 'I think I ought to tell you, sir, that there is a wolf in the laundry.' My father said, 'Nonsense,' but we all went down to the laundry and looked over the top of the half-door. It was late and rather dark, but we could see a creature there, running up and down and snarling. My father said: 'I think it's only a dog, but he seems very fierce; leave him there for tonight, and I will get the police in the morning.' I thought I had gone to bed and to sleep, still vaguely knowing that there was a restless animal shut up not far away. Then I dreamt that I woke suddenly, with an unspeakable shock, to the consciousness that someone was lying in bed beside me. I put my hand out and touched the soft naked shoulders of a woman. My heart stood absolutely still with fear, for I knew with complete certainty that this was the spirit of a werewolf woman, which had been inhabiting the body of the wolf in the laundry; and that she had now come to take possession of me. She lay beside me in the bed, a little, soft-skinned, small-boned creature. She took my left hand and began to draw it across herself, very slowly and softly, but

quite irresistibly; and I knew that if she got it right across and laid my hand on her heart, I should be hers for ever. I could neither move nor speak, and my hand was being pulled further and further across her; when suddenly I was able to make the sign of the cross with my right hand; and I woke trembling to see the blessed dawn coming in the window...

Elaborate as this story seems, the visual, auditory and tactile elements that go to make it up are very simple. Note that the dreamer does not actually see the werewolf woman, she touches her in the dark and what she finds herself touching is 'a little, soft-skinned, small-boned creature'; she does not see the wolf in the laundry, but sees and hears something 'rather like a snarling dog'. Neither of those images, taken on its own, is anything but ordinary. Gwen had probably touched just such a body in the dark many times – the body of her younger sister, Margaret, who sometimes crept into the bed beside her (and quite possibly had on some occasion reached out and taken her left hand). She had also many times seen and heard a snarling dog – it might have been her own dog, Sancho. But it is the context, and the juxtaposition of these familiar images which changes everything. The story requires but a single line to set it up: 'I ought to tell you, sir, that there is a wolf in the laundry' – and *then* when the next image is a snarling creature it *has* to be a wolf, when the next is a small body in the bed beside you it has to be a werewolf woman.

In such ways, using what amounts almost to a kind of elementary dream Lego, the dreamer can construct any number of extraordinary scenarios – through which she might (or might not) introduce herself to new emotions. Sometimes it will be random, but sometimes it will not. Here is an example that perhaps has more immediate relevance to human social life. In about 1550, St Teresa of Avila had a vision – a dream, or in this case it may have been a waking trance – in which she imagined herself visited by an angel:

> In his hands I saw a long golden spear and at the end of the iron tip I seemed to see a point of fire. With this he seemed to pierce my heart repeatedly so that it penetrated to my entrails. When he drew it out I thought he was drawing them out with it, and he left me completely afire with a great love of God. The pain was so great that I screamed aloud, but simultaneously felt such an infinite sweetness that I wished the pain would last eternally.[5]

Few people would question that what St Teresa is describing here is the experience that most – but perhaps not all of us – know as the experience that accompanies sexual union: not just the experience of physiological orgasm, but of the intense love felt for a sexual partner. But there is every reason to suppose that St Teresa – who entered a convent at the age of 16 – never had a sexual partner in real life. How then could she have imagined a situation so true to the real thing?

I think we can be fairly sure that she could *not* have imagined it if she had been totally sexually inexperienced; but no doubt she was not. Most children experiment, innocently enough, with their own bodies, and the genital sensations were probably quite familiar to her. What was new in her 'vision', however, was the context she herself gave to those sensations, because now – probably for the first time in her life – her ecstasy was apparently being brought on by a male partner, the spear-carrying angel. Thus, in her imagination, by bringing together two otherwise familiar images from memory, she created the very conditions under which she could have a quite new experience – the experience of sexual love. I would suggest with all seriousness that on account of this vision St Teresa (if she had not lived as an isolated nun) might indeed have become a better natural psychologist: better at understanding, from the inside, the love-life of other human beings. She herself put something of the same construction on it, though as it happens the other way around.

> So gentle is this wooing which takes place between God and the soul that if anyone think I am lying, I pray God in his goodness, to grant him some experience of it.

Yet where did the idea for this particular conjunction of images arise from (and we could ask the same question about any other dream)? It might have been merely fortuitous, though that seems unlikely. It might have been prompted by a picture she had seen, a story she had read, or something she had heard of from her schoolfriends or her nurse. But it might (and I do not think this possibility should be rejected out of hand) have been nothing less than the flowering of an 'instinctive' fantasy – a story planted in every embryonic human soul to teach people a lesson in psychology that otherwise they might not ever learn.

The role of biological determination should not, however, be overstressed. C. G. Jung did indeed claim that dreams have an instinctive base: 'We do not dream', he said, 'we are dreamed' – as if nature herself is our hypnotist, our dream-director, guiding us along paths laid down long ago in our evolutionary history. Sometimes the evidence for some complex archetypal programming is too strong to be ignored. But for a child on the way to becoming a psychologist, the 'biological directives', if they exist at all, might actually be very simple: no more, I suspect, than – just as in childhood play – to put *oneself* at the centre of everything one sees (or hears of) happening to other people, and sometimes, of course, to go over one's own life again.

It is, I think, no accident that the majority of dreams are actually quite undramatic, being concerned simply with imitation, role-playing, and the acting-out of relatively ordinary situations. No accident either that as children grow up towards maturity, their dreams become increasingly oriented towards exploring those *social* situations which in waking life prey on the child's mind. Werewolves, St Joan, swimming rivers with a dagger in your mouth may be a part of it, but they are not the most common kind of dream; and no one could argue that those are the areas of feeling a child most needs to explore. They are, perhaps, the kind of dreams that people think worth telling (and no doubt such self-selection of dream-stories accounts in part for some of the more florid theories of what dreams are for). But much that could count more immediately towards a child's education goes unrecorded. David Foulkes made an extensive study of 'unselected' dreams, obtained from children immediately after they had been deliberately awakened at random times. Here, as a contrast to Gwen Raverat and St Teresa, are samples of the dreams of a young American girl, around the age of twelve.[6]

It was a nice night before Easter and we had company over at our house and nobody would get in bed. There was a big fight and everybody was crying. There were two boys that were in the bedroom and they were throwing a bunny back and forth to each other. And then another girl was in the living room crying. And a girl popped another girl's balloon, and then she got mad at her, and they started having a fight. I was kind of mad. Nobody would go to bed and I was trying to get them to bed.

We were in this car with a friend of mine, they were taking us home, and her mother was French and she had a French accent. And something was in the street that was mine, a necklace, and we stopped and this other girl got out to get it. And her father just drove off, and left her there ... left her there standing out in the street all alone. I was just sitting in the car. We were all looking at each other and wondering ... and I felt kind of angry toward the father.

I had a dream that I had to do a dance in front of a whole bunch of people. And I had different socks, and I had great big holes in the bottom of my socks. And I didn't know it. I looked and I saw them, and I felt embarrassed.

Nothing so extraordinary there, and yet each of these dreams is arguably a significant exercise in human feeling – practice for what it feels like to be someone else.

Why is this power of dreams not recognized? There is reason to think it has been in the past, and in other cultures it still is.

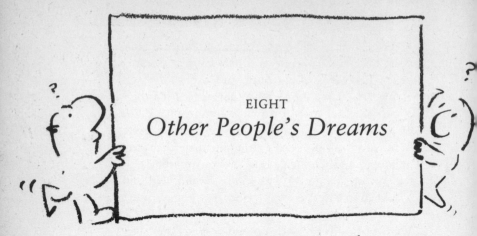

EIGHT
Other People's Dreams

In T. S. Eliot's poem *The Waste Land*[1] the typist comes home, lights her stove, lays out her supper from a tin, eats it, and waits indifferently for the carbuncular small-house-agent's-clerk to come and ravish her. Somebody is watching. Who? It is none other than the old prophet of classical mythology, Tiresias. 'I Tiresias, though blind, throbbing between two lives, / Old man with wrinkled female breasts ... perceived the scene and foretold the rest.' Tiresias is Mr Universal Experience; he has been himself a typist, a house agent, a man, a woman. 'I Tiresias have foresuffered all / Enacted on this same divan or bed;' and there is nothing anyone can teach him, especially about sex.

It was indeed in the matter of sex that Tiresias first earned his reputation as a seer. Ovid tells of a lover's quarrel between the gods Jupiter and Juno. Jupiter maintained that women get much more pleasure from sexual intercourse than men do, but Juno said the opposite was true. The problem was, how could either of them *know*? There was as it happened only one person who could claim to have tried out both the male and female role, and that was Tiresias. One day, when out for a walk, Tiresias had seen two snakes in the act of coupling. He had killed the female with his staff, and had immediately been changed into a woman. For seven years he had lived as a celebrated prostitute. Then he came across a second pair of snakes, but this time he killed the male, and was transformed back to his former manhood. Tiresias, being qualified as no one else was by his personal experience, was summoned by the gods to settle their dispute. His judgement on the matter was precise: 'If the parts of love pleasure be counted as ten, thrice three go to women, one only to men.' Juno was so enraged at being proved wrong that she condemned Tiresias to eternal blindness. Jupiter compensated him by granting him inward vision and the power of prophecy. Tiresias from that point on did not look back: he travelled in and out of every kind of life, and moved freely between the upper and the lower worlds.

I doubt that any human being this side of mythology has achieved such a level of universal insight. But the *idea* of Tiresias, of a man who is empowered by his own personal experience to understand everything from the inside, is present in almost every human culture – and not represented always as a myth. Tiresias belongs to the tradition of 'wise men'. – diviners, doctors, healers – who today are often classed together as 'shamans', and they are found from Siberia to Amazonia, and from Neanderthal times until the present day. Shamans are individuals who, in theory at least, have suffered every conceivable kind of human trauma, and therefore can see by the light of their own experience further and deeper than any ordinary men. They are, as it were, supernatural psychologists – able to read, as Tiresias could, the 'meanings ambushed under all they see'.[2]

To become a shaman a man or woman must always undergo a process of initiation. Sexual transformation is only part of it, although it is sometimes an important part. In Northern Siberia, for example, a Chuckchee initiate 'throws down the lasso of the reindeer herdsman and the harpoon of the seal hunter, and takes to the needle and the skin scraper... He loses his masculine strength and acquires instead the helplessness of a woman'[3]; he becomes a 'soft man', and may take a husband, with whom he makes love as a woman. But change of sex is symbolic of change in general, and the process of initiation may take a wide variety of forms: the focus, however, is always on metamorphosis, on the breaking of boundaries. Sometimes it involves a period of illness: 'Before I commenced to shamanize, I lay sick for a whole year. The sickness that forced me to this path showed itself in a swelling of my body and frequent spells of fainting.'[4] Sometimes a period of enforced hardship or pain: 'She was hung up to some tent poles planted in the snow and left there for five days. When the five days were at an end, she was taken down and shot ... using a stone instead of a leaden bullet in order that she might still retain connection with the earth.'[5] But almost always, either in addition to, or as a substitute for, real experience, the initiate is expected to undertake 'dream journeys' where in a state of trance or ecstasy he confronts demons, makes spirit allies, dies and is reborn.

These trances or dreams, which are generally regarded as the chief source of the shaman's power, may come about spontaneously, or be brought on with the help of hallucinogenic drugs. But however they arise, their content and form are *culturally prescribed*. The 'way of the shaman' is well known even to those who do not attempt to follow it, and neither the social group nor the initiate himself will recognize his initiation as successful unless he has taken the right road. Sometimes, as among the Yanamamo of Brazil, the initiation is validated at the time by elder shamans who act out in public the drama that is supposed to be going on inside the initiate's head while he himself remains in a drug-induced stupor. Among the Buryats of Eastern Siberia, the initiate may even be made to take an examination later on to test whether he has in fact acquired the requisite spiritual experience.

No one knows the origins of shamanism. The practices have become overlaid with a welter of religious and political interpretation, and original motives and meanings have been distorted or altogether lost. None the less the central tenet has probably remained essentially unchanged: the belief that the shaman, as a result of his trials and visions, achieves an unprecedented degree of inner knowledge. He travels to and beyond the boundaries of human experience, and comes back as someone with first-hand experience of the psychic world. Now, when he has to solve a problem, he will know where to go: 'Will this man catch fish if he fishes in that river?' – the shaman will dive into the river and ask the fish. 'What is the cure for this woman's sickness?' – the shaman will ask the spirits who are making her ill.

Much of it is, of course, in practice phoney, and both shamans and their clients may be well aware that most shamans do not, in fact, possess the powers they claim. True enough, a man who has himself been sick will by that token have greater insight into sickness, and a man who has dreamed of being a fish may even have a better understanding of where the fish have gone. But in most cases there is no longer any simple one-to-one connection between the shaman's experience and his particular powers of prophecy or insight.

At the heart of shamanism there still lies, however, a kernel of psychological *realpolitik*. Shamanic initiations are designed to tackle a genuine psychological and ontological dilemma. 'How shall I know the way of all things?' wrote Lao Tzu, ' – by what is inside me.' But what *is* inside me? Only what I have experienced for myself: and that in principle cannot be everything there is. No matter how effective the natural strategies that human beings have for extending their personal experience – among them the strategies I have discussed in the last chapters: play, parental teasing, naturally occurring dreams – there are bound to be areas of experience that individuals have no access to. Shamanic initiations, especially the dream journey, provide, as it were, a crash course in personal experience: a thousand years of human living rolled into a day.

The idea is sensible enough. Yet in our own culture shamanism, as such, has evidently all but died. Admittedly pockets of the old tradition persist in other guises: notably in the world of psychoanalysis where the training of an analyst closely resembles a traditional initiation, with its emphasis on transformation of the self, confrontation with dark forces, sexual confusion and so on – all of it guided by an elder shaman who has trod the thorny path before. But such practices remain at the margin of our own society. At first sight it seems that Western culture neither encourages nor recognizes the role of the dream journey, let alone prescribes a particular regime of fantasy.

For asking questions like that one..
Say WISE MAN-
what are
MINDS
for?
HOW TO BE CONSCIOUS

In fact, I believe the opposite is true. Whereas in primitive societies, initiation is limited to the chosen few, in our society it is open to almost everyone. To the extent that the purpose of the shamanic journey is to provide a man or woman, who might otherwise have limited experience, with extraordinary opportunities for exploring his own soul, we have invented substitutes so powerful and so prevalent that we no longer recognize them for what they are. I am talking of institutionalized fantasy: books, plays, music, paintings, films.

It will not, I think, be clear exactly what I mean. I can only ask you to consider your own case. How do you – the product, I expect, entirely of a Western culture – compare in your understanding of the human psyche with, say, a Yanamamo shaman from the Amazonian forest? Who has the greater knowledge of the spiritual struggles that go in human beings? Which of you has the deeper insight into sex, war, family politics, crime, etc., and has ranged furthest across the frontiers that separate individual people? I do not doubt that you have. For, unlike the Yanamamo shaman, you have, let's say, travelled with Defoe, loved with Shakespeare, sung along with Verdi, laughed with Runyan, and seen the world through the eyes of Rembrandt or van Gogh. From earliest youth you have been party to a culture which in effect, and maybe by design, drums into every one of us the accumulated experience of a multitude of other people's lives.

Suppose a Yanamamo Indian – or for that matter Jupiter or Juno – were to visit a major Western capital: London, Paris, Moscow, Rome (it might be Tokyo or Delhi, but those are not places I have been). Everywhere he would see evidence of a society that goes far out of its way to lay on vicarious experience for its citizens: public games, circuses, cinema, fairgrounds, concert halls, art galleries, theatres, libraries, newspapers, romantic magazines. Huge amounts of time, money and human genius are devoted to it. The opera house, the gallery, the library are the finest buildings in town. Public squares have as many statues to artists and writers as they do to generals. A single painting may fetch the price of a factory, a film cost as much as large hospital ... He might note, too, that even without going outside their doors the citizens of Britain spend an average of five hours a day sitting – entranced? – before a television screen. Indeed, a visitor who came to observe us with an open mind might well conclude that here is a culture obsessed with the business of experience-gathering. But more than that, a culture that has developed the most astonishing techniques for doing it: ways of communicating emotion between total strangers.

Yet what is it all really for? A standard answer is that the chief function of dramatic entertainment is catharsis – that it is a means of taking emotional exercise, and of working off emotional energies in a controlled way. But that I am sure is not the half of it. There may indeed be times when people need the not unfamiliar experience of having a good laugh or a good cry simply to get it out of their system – or perhaps merely to remind themselves that they are human. But to suppose that is all there is to the emotional experience aroused by events on stage or screen or page, would be as blinkered as to suppose that being hung up from a tent-pole for five days, or undergoing a trip on mescalin does no more than take the pressure off the shaman's nerves. Far more important must be the role it has in extending experience into unfamiliar areas and so of examining for oneself the critical events that move other people to grief, jealousy, triumph or whatever.

How does it work, for example, with literary fiction? Charles Dickens wrote a story, *The Old Curiosity Shop*. It concerns a little girl, Nell, and her grandfather who, forced by debt to sell their shop, wander about the country suffering great hardships and pursued by heartless creditors. At last they find a haven in a cottage beside a village church. Just as a rich relation is about to reach them, little Nell, worn out by her troubles, dies. The novel was published in serial form in 1841. As the story moved to its tragic climax Dickens was inundated by his readers with 'imploring letters recommending poor little Nell to mercy'. Waiting crowds at a New York pier shouted to an incoming vessel, 'Is little Nell dead?'. 'She is dead,' the captain called back from the bridge, and a wave of shock and grief spread through the city. In London, when the blow fell, the great historian Thomas Carlyle professed himself utterly overcome. Lord Jeffrey was found by a friend in his library with his head bowed upon the table; he raised it and she saw that his eyes were bathed in tears. 'I had no idea that you had any bad news or cause of grief,' she said, 'or I would not have come. Is anyone dead?' 'Yes, indeed,' he replied.[6]

Now this is what Dickens wrote in the novel.

> If there be any who have never known the blank
> that follows death – the weary void – the sense of
> desolation that will come upon the strongest minds,
> when something familiar and beloved is missed at
> every turn ... if there be any who have not known
> this and proved it by their own experience, they can
> never faintly guess how, for many days, the old man

pined and moped away the time, and wandered here and there as seeking something, and had no comfort.

But suppose Lord Jeffrey, for one, had not 'known it and proved it by his own experience'? Could he 'faintly guess' the old man's feelings? The effect of Dickens's writing was precisely to belie what he himself had written: for if any reader had not felt those feelings before, he surely had by the time Dickens had finished with him. For thousands of people Dickens was midwife to the very sense of desolation he described.

The Chinese sage Lin Shu said this of books: 'People in a book at once become my nearest and dearest relations. When they are in difficulties I fall into despair; when they are successful I am triumphant. I am no longer a human being, but a puppet whom the author dangles on his strings.'[7] Who does not know for themselves the power of books, plays, films to lead us on? How many of our first encounters with human feelings came that way? One of the first real fears I remember was the fear of the crocodile in *Peter Pan* (at the age of four I had to be taken from the theatre to recover). One of my first loves was for Natasha in *War and Peace*, whose name I inscribed in carefully copied Cyrillic script on my pillowcase at school. A print of Munch's painting, *The Cry*, was my model for adolescent anguish. Slavery was Paul Robeson's songs. Tension was *High Noon*. And so it still goes on. Until last week, when I read *Empire of the Sun*, I had not thought that *that* was how it must have felt to be a Japanese prisoner of war.

But wait a minute. Natasha did not even exist, let alone did she ever have anything to do with *me*.

Robeson was never actually a slave. *High Noon*, for all I know, took place on a Hollywood set at ten past three. How is it that the illusion can be so effective? We *are* puppets, and for centuries the techniques of the puppeteers have been developed and refined.

Dramatic entertainment is not a new invention, but it has been brought to new peaks of sophistication in the culture to which you and I belong. Consider – as a stock example, but one which none the less will make my point – a performance of *Romeo and Juliet* on the London stage. How is the effect achieved? It begins with the theatre as a place: a temple-like building, totally separate in style and mood from the city streets outside. We are ushered into the sanctum by uniformed attendants. No one here is quite himself. The atmosphere is charged with expectation. Already, before the performance has commenced, we are being softened up: given the premedication that precedes the operation on our minds. The lights go out, the curtain rises. Hush! The chorus speaks:

> ...From forth the fatal loins of these two foes
> A pair of star-crossed lovers take their life;
> Whose misadventured piteous overthrows
> Do with their death bury their parents' strife.

We are told from the start just where this story will be leading. We are forewarned, but not forearmed at all: for our knowledge of where the star-crossed lovers' love must end, only makes their commitment to each other more pathetic. It is a trick that will be repeated through the play – most tellingly at the point where Romeo, not knowing *as we know* that she is sleeping, believes that Juliet has already died.

So the drama has begun. The chorus, our only point of direct connection with the players – the only one of them who speaks to *us* – departs and delivers us to the 'two hours traffick of our stage'. In the darkness of the theatre we enter now a state that is in several ways quite like dream-sleep, surrendering ourselves to a make-believe world of quarrelling families, masked balls, meddling friars, apothecary's drugs. We ourselves do not speak, do not move. Just like the state of dreaming, it is as though our bodies have been temporarily paralysed. But however slack our bodies have become, we have become *in mind* a part of the action on the stage.

But in what sense have we become *a part*? One thing is certain: we ourselves are not present in the story. In that respect the drama is quite different from a true dream. Dreams are participatory, first person fantasies. We figure in our dreams and interact with the development. The things that happen, happen directly to ourselves or to characters to whom we feel ourselves personally related. But here in the theatre we are no more than spectators. Why should we feel ourselves in any way *involved* with the fate of these two strangers on the stage?

Let us be clear that in real life we do not feel involved with everybody. It depends in general on our having some genuine relationship to them. The theatre-goer may have read that very afternoon of an earthquake in Mexico that killed five thousand real live human beings, a thousand Juliets among them. Yet most likely not one of their deaths affected him emotionally. He was not related to those deaths in Mexico; yet here, strangely, he *is*. For the play has persuaded him not only to suspend his disbelief, but to harbour a whole set of new beliefs. He is under an illusion: the illusion that he himself has the right or even the duty to feel himself involved. Indeed the key to the effectiveness of drama (and literary fiction) lies precisely in this: that it cun-

ningly creates the conditions which foster the illusion that a personal relationship exists between
the spectators and the actors. The people in a book,
the people in a play, become at once 'our nearest
and dearest relations'.

How is this illusory relationship stage-managed?
The curtain rises, and there on stage are characters
of whom initially we know nothing whatsoever.
The first task of the dramatist must be quite simply
to provide us with background information – but
without us realizing the extent to which we are
being set up. Thus Romeo is introduced before he
ever sets foot on stage as a subject of worried conversation between his cousin and his parents.
Juliet's character emerges in a three-way discussion
between Juliet, her mother and her nurse – and it is
as clever a way of saying 'This is Juliet Capulet,
(14), unmarried, trouble brewing', as only Shakespeare could contrive.

Yet personal details and hints about the plot are
not, of course, necessarily enough to get us, the
audience, actively involved. What is required is that
we should believe ourselves in some way *needed* –
so that our fear, our jealousy or anger can have
some point. But how, of all things, can the dramatist suggest *their* need for *us*? Part of it will rest with
the nature of the character: a child, a girl, an
unworldly person – a 'vulnerable' or 'insufficient'
personality – will have the best chance of persuad-
ing us that there is space beside them for ourselves.
Think of some of Shakespeare's other heroes,
Richard II, Lear, Hamlet; or of Dickens's Oliver
Twist, Pickwick, Micawber – hopeless cases all of
them and desperately in need of a (our?) helping
hand.

But much of the effect will still rely on presentation. In some way a sense of intimacy has to be hinted at: the sense not only that we know them, but (if they only knew it!) they know us. One of the most obvious and effective devices for bringing this about is to make us privy to thoughts and events which no one *except* an intimate of the character *could* share with her. Thus nurses, mothers, cousins, etc. become essential to the structure of a play not just because they are an excuse for imparting information, but because they are a way of showing us our own relationship to that information: a relationship of trust, familiarity, responsibility.

Confidences are revealed, precisely to make us feel that we ourselves are confidantes. Yet while we are privileged to share Juliet's discussions with her nurse, we are more privileged still to hear her discussions with no one but herself. Indeed, when it can be used, it is the private soliloquy that will prove the most winning trick of all. Juliet stands at her window, speaking, so she thinks, to the night air and no one else. 'Ay me...', she says. And the fact that we are with her in uttering that single sigh is enough to put us under an obligation to the end.

Dramatic effects do not just happen: they happen because there are artists among us who know how to make them happen. And whether it is in theatre, literature, painting or music, these artists are heirs to a long tradition of experimentation and research. The tricks of stagecraft in particular have been known and exploited since classical times, and have been developed continuously since. Yet it has been in the last fifty years, with the invention of cine-film and television, that the techniques for forwarding experience have really come into their own – bringing us closer than human beings have ever been to the full possibilities of a 'shared dream'.

The parallels between films and dreams have often been remarked on. In particular, film has a unique power to create the illusion of intimacy. In a book or on stage, intimacy has to be worked for, and requires from the audience a degree of willing cooperation. But on screen it is there for the taking. The use of close-up, point-of-view perspectives, voice-over commentary, can indeed make the film uncannily like one of our own first-person dreams: a dream in which we are involved bodily as well as mentally.

True, the cinema as a place does not have the aura of a theatre. Nor does a film, as a perform-ance, have the quality of danger that a stage per-formance does. None the less it is cinema films which for most people in the world today come closest to making a reality of the culturally pre-scribed dream-journey. I remember one film above all from when I was a boy, de Sica's *The Bicycle Thieves*, which tells the story of an impoverished Italian workman who has his bicycle stolen, loses his job, and wanders the streets with his young son looking for the thieves. It was shown in Italian with English subtitles; I was six and scarcely old enough to read the words. Yet the emotional lesson con-veyed by the images alone was complete, and the film became my model of how poverty, unfairness and desperation must feel. I do not believe that Tiresias himself was ever offered that kind of opportunity.

The opportunities are there in our society. How are they being used? Let me voice at once some res-ervations. For a start, I believe that we have been spoiled. As the techniques for involving an audi-ence in fantasy relationships have grown, so has our appetite and our demand for it. In a free market of the kind we live in now, that appetite will be endlessly indulged.

Consider this: now that our appetite has been whetted for vicarious adventure, we may no longer be content with the fictional offerings of the theatre or cinema – we want to see the dramas of real life. A young Russian is refused permission to marry his American fiancée: 'Red Romeo in heartbreak love tryst with US Juliet', shout the newspapers. But these are real people, not actors, whose lives are being served up in the form of drama. Actors are professionals, it is their job to entertain us by playing out intimate scenes in public; but it is not the job of any private citizen to do the same. Increasingly, however, in our greed for emotional involvement we let ourselves 'kidnap' ordinary people and manage their lives as if they *were* on stage. We demand intimacy even when it is not offered. And now the very techniques which a writer/director uses to introduce a stranger to his audience are turned against the private citizen who wishes to remain a stranger: an AIDS victim, the mother of a test-tube baby, a homosexual priest, the father of a missing child.

I am not saying the process of involvement does not work. The joy a loyal subject feels at the birth of a royal baby, or the anxiety over the outcome of a police search for a child, are genuine emotions and may well be genuinely educational. Likewise the horror at seeing a black kid shot down by Botha's soldiers, or anger at the way an adulterous husband is behaving, or even perhaps interest in a Casablanca sex-change. We're learning – learning about the possibilities of human feelings – all the time, and maybe we would be poorer psychologists and hence poorer citizens without it. We live in an

I suppose this teaches you about grief, joy, jealousy and TRIUMPH in a way that no NOVEL ever could..

MATCH of the DAY

increasingly complex world, and need increasingly complex experience to round out our understanding of the other human creatures in it. But when part of what we are learning is that other people are no more than fodder for our fantasies, the lesson is ambiguous to say the least.

What is more, beyond a certain point we are not doing ourselves any good by indulging this appetite for vicarious experience of all kinds. Instead of being a means of helping us lead richer lives in the real world, it can become a substitute for the real world, or take us up side-alleys that have little or nothing to do with human relationships. As the opportunities for indulging in fantasy relationships grow – whether under pressure from the entertainment industry or through this process of cashing in on real life drama – we are at risk of forgetting what it is all about. Whereas in the past, our involvement with drama has been a means of extending our understanding of the real people around us, our present-day absorption with packaged fictions may indeed be self-defeating. Illusory relationships become a substitute for real life ones. Experiential 'kicks' replace genuinely useful psychological adventures. It is one thing to spend two hours of the night dreaming, another to spend five hours glued to a television screen. The techniques of the modern media can and do provide us with an artificial 'superstimulus'.

There is a more worrying issue still, and that is the near certainty that we are being manipulated by those very social institutions which do so much to extend our experiential range. No regime of education is ever free of ideology. Just as a shamanic culture lays down the course that its wise men must follow, so our civilized Western society lays down the kinds of experience that its citizens should be exposed to.

I talked of a culturally prescribed regime of fantasy. But who does the prescribing? It can be argued that we ourselves do: a society is no more than the sum of its parts and we get the culture we deserve. But that is too easy an answer. The fact is that very few of us are in control. We hand over responsibility to other people — media moguls, censors, politicians — and as Plato noted nearly two and a half thousand years ago when he set out his prescription for an Ideal State, such 'guardians' have a state duty to take a close interest in the arts:

We soon reap the fruits of literature in life, and pro-
longed indulgence in any form of literature leaves its
mark on the moral nature of a man.[8]

Accordingly, in Plato's *Republic* it was strictly for-
bidden to portray, for example, women abusing
their husbands, women in sickness or love or child-
birth, people complaining of misfortune, slaves
answering back, bad or cowardly characters,
madmen, and even horses neighing and bulls bel-
lowing – in fact, anything other than 'men of courage, self-control, independence and religious
principle'.

Autocracies of the kind Plato recommended tend
to rule by prohibition. Free-market democracies,
such as ours in theory is, do the opposite. Anything
goes in our society: but especially anything that (*a*)
makes money, (*b*) encourages self-interest, (*c*)
covertly defends the status quo. True, the arts may
flourish over the heads of such political or econ-
omic forces. In drama and literature the great
themes that have always concerned people do
indeed survive and re-emerge: *West Side Story* – a
modern Romeo and Juliet; *E.T.* – a re-enactment of
the Christ story; *2001* – a space-age Odyssey. Their
message is so strong and so much wanted, that they
will not go away. But alongside them, and increasingly dominant as film and television take a hold,
are themes of quite another kind.

Our society does not ban films that show women
abusing men, or slaves answering back: it simply
swamps them with more merchantable products
which show women being abused, or men made
slaves. It does not ban representations of the mis-
fortunes of war, because for every one there will be
a hundred – a hundred times more popular – that

show war to be a hero's work.

I imagined an Amazonian Indian visiting our culture. I imagined him impressed by the techniques we have developed for exploring the length and breadth of human feeling. And the end result of these two thousand years of our having access to other people's dreams? One result is you. Another is a young American infantryman who, having killed a man, is surprised because *he feels the way that anyone might feel*: 'I felt sorry. I don't know why I felt sorry. John Wayne never felt sorry.'[9] It has been said that there is no great truth of which the opposite is not also a great truth. The truth is that the culture which raises us up, can bring us down.

NINE

Where Are We Going?

Confirmation of Darwin's theory of the origin of coral atolls came late. 'I wish', Darwin had written in 1881, 'that some doubly rich millionaire would take it into his head to have borings made in some of the Pacific or Indian atolls, and bring back cores from a depth of 500 or 600 feet.'[1] Not until 1952 was Darwin's wish fulfilled. The coral at the site near Bikini atoll proved to be nearly a mile deep, and beneath it, even deeper than Darwin had anticipated, was the black rock of a submerged volcano. The millionaire behind the project was the American Atomic Energy Commission. The reason for it was not to test Darwin's theory but to prepare the way for a nuclear explosion.

Much closer to Tahiti, on Muroroa atoll, the French government began testing nuclear weapons in 1966. More than eighty nuclear devices – atom bombs, hydrogen bombs and neutron bombs – have been exploded there in the last twenty years, and Muroroa is now, in the words of the chief French technician, 'a radioactive Gruyère cheese'. Cracks have appeared in the island's structure, from which plutonium leaks out into the ocean and will persist as an active poison for the next 25 million years.

When an atom bomb goes off on a Pacific island, this is what it is like:

> Albatrosses will fly for days, skimming a few inches above the surface of the water... Beautiful creatures. Watching them is a wonder... We were standing around waiting for this bomb to go off, which we had been told was a very small one... And the countdown comes in over the radio... And suddenly I could see all these birds... And they were smoking. Their feathers were on fire. And they were doing cartwheels... They were being consumed by the heat. Their feathers were on fire. They were blinded. And so far there had been no shock, none of blast damage we talk about when we discuss the effects of nuclear weapons. Instead there were just these smoking, twisting, hideously contorted birds crashing into things. (Interview with an observer of a test at Christmas Island.)[2]

And when an atom bomb goes off over a city, this is what it is like:

> The appearance of the people was ... well, they all had skin blackened by burns. They had no hair because their hair was burned, and at a glance you couldn't tell whether you were looking at them front or back. They held their arms bent like this ... and their skin − not only their hands, but on their faces and bodies, too − hung down... Wherever I walked I met these people. Many of them died along the road − I can still picture them in my mind − like walking ghosts. They didn't look like people of this world. They had a special way of walking − very slowly... I myself was one of them. (Interview with a survivor of Hiroshima.)[3]

And this is how men talk about atomic weapons, a speech by Senator McMahon in 1952:

> Some people used to claim that A-bombs, numbered in the thousands or tens of thousands, were beyond our reach. I am here to report to the Senate and the American people that the atomic bottlenecks are being broken. There is virtually no limit and no limiting factor upon the number of A-bombs which the United States can manufacture, given time and given a decision to proceed all out... We must have atomic weapons to use in the heights of the sky and the depths of the sea; we must have them to use above the ground, on the ground, and below the ground.[4]

In terms of the story I have been telling about the evolution of human social intelligence and the capacity for insight, something has gone very badly wrong. Alone in the animal world we are capable of knowing what we are doing, and the effect our own actions may be having upon other human beings. Such insight and imagination *ought* to provide the greatest restraint possible on human acts of cruelty, or blindness or indifference to the suffering of others. Yet again and again, human relationships go up in smoke. After six million years of human evolution, there are just, it sometimes seems, these smoking, twisting, hideously contorted human bodies crashing into one another.

Does the explanation lie in ignorance? Is it possible that when people behave cruelly to other human beings, they simply 'know not what they do'? There are, as we have seen, both natural and cultural safeguards against experiential ignorance, but I would not claim that any of the avenues to human knowledge I outlined earlier are foolproof.

In any society there will be people – and they may, especially in our own society, be powerful people – who simply have no clear picture of the effect their actions or policies may have on other human beings: a Minister for Employment who has never (even in fantasy) himself been out of work, a Catholic priest who has never experienced the tensions of the marriage-bed, a queen who has never eaten anything but cake. We are not ruled by 'wise men'. The highest offices of State may be held, as Bertrand Russell put it, by sets of 'official gentlemen, living luxurious lives, mostly stupid, and all without imagination or heart'.[5]

Yet while such personal lack of human expertise may well lead to insensitivity and idiocy in dealing with others, it is unlikely of itself to lead to outright cruelty. There can be no human beings so deprived – or so cosseted – in their own lives, that they do not know the basic alphabet of human feelings. No one can suppose, for example, that the Nazis were simply incapable of understanding the suffering of their victims in the concentration camps. On this point there exists, as ironic testimony to Hitler's sensitivity to suffering, the evidence of his Animal Protection Act of 1933, drafted by Goering, signed by Hitler: 'It shall be prohibited unnecessarily to torture or brutally to ill-treat an animal ... To ill-treat an animal means to cause it pain. Ill-treatment is deemed brutal when it is inspired by a lack of feeling.'[6] No one can suppose either – to take an example nearer home – that the captain of HMS *Conqueror* was simply ignorant of what it might feel like to be drowned when at the beginning of the Falklands War he sunk the battleship *General Belgrano*, with the loss of more than 300 young Argentinian lives.

No, when people hurt other people, deliberately, knowingly, there is something other than personal ignorance behind it. It is seldom if ever that such people are incapable of knowing just what they do, it is that there are circumstances under which people will choose to believe that *here* they are *not doing anything of human consequence at all*.

The inner world of other people is invisible to the outer eye. To reach into someone else's mind requires an act of imagination on our part: we have, as natural psychologists, to 'smell out' what other people may be feeling, to construct it on the basis of how *we* should feel if we were them. It is this ability to imagine other people as versions of ourselves which human beings are – or should be – good at. But the very fact that our understanding of others requires this intermediate act of imaginative reconstruction, creates the space for failure. For insight into others becomes potentially an *option*, not a necessity, to human beings. And people may refuse it.

Failure occurs, with more or less objectionable consequences, in every sphere of life. Certainly it is not only in the context of war that the option of 'dehumanizing' other human beings makes a mockery of natural human relationships. The madness of war may emerge within a human family, between friends, on a miners' picket line, or on the streets of Palermo, Belfast or New York. For a child battered to death by its own parents, a woman raped, a 'scab' spurned by his friends, or a Protestant kneecapped by the IRA, the human capacity to feel with others has proved as shallow an evolutionary creation as it was for any of the individual victims of Hiroshima or Belsen.

War none the less is something special; special by

its scale and its astonishing impersonality. I have said that imagination may be fragile, but it is not so fragile as to explain why human beings as soldiers behave the way they do: killing others almost wholly without consideration, for no personal gain, with no personal grudge.

I have to remind myself of what can happen. This interview was recorded with a veteran of Vietnam:[7]

> *Question*: How many men aboard each chopper?
> *Answer*: Five of us. And we landed next to the village, and we all got on line and we started walking toward the village. And there was one man, one gook, in the shelter, and he was all huddled up down in there, and the man called out and said there's a gook over there.
> *Q*: How old a man was this? I mean was this a fighting man or an older man?
> *A*: An older man. And the man said there's a gook over here, and then Sergeant Mitchell hollered back and said shoot him...
> *Q*: Okay. Then what?
> *A*: So we started to gather them up, more people ... and we dropped a hand grenade in there with them.
> *Q*: Men, women and children?
> *A*: Men, women and children ... and babies...
> *Q*: Why did you do it?
> *A*: Because I felt like I was ordered to do it...
> *Q*: They weren't begging, or saying 'No ... no...'
> *A*: Right. They were begging and saying, 'No, no.' And the mothers was hugging their children.

Let's say that for most ordinary people there is a simple question they would ask themselves before they would blow up a mother and her children. It's this: '*I* wonder how my actions may be affecting *you*.' How do you *stop* a man asking or answering that question? How do you stop a man imagining? Alas, there are at least four weak points in the simple imaginative chain from 'I' to 'you', and techniques, deliberately exploited in the training of a soldier, exist for breaking every one of them.

'I'

Central to the conditioning of a soldier is the destruction of his sense of 'I'. The existence of a 'self-concept' is something I referred to earlier as one of the most elementary evidences of consciousness in animals and men. By the age of 18 months a normal human child has begun to differentiate himself as a separate self, feeling and thinking independently of other human beings. It is through discovering how he feels that he begins to imagine that others may feel similarly: his 'I' becomes the model for the 'I' in others.

Basic training as practised in the American Army, and in every other army in the world, is designed deliberately to undermine the sense of 'I'. Peter Bourne, an American psychiatrist, described the procedures at Boot Camp, where recruits were trained to serve in Vietnam:

> The early weeks of training are characterized by physical and verbal abuse, humiliation, and a constant discounting and discrediting of everything which serves to characterize him as an individual. His head is shaved, his ability to think independently is scorned, and every moment of his day is minutely programmed and scheduled.[8]

The effect – sometimes clearly the intention – of such training is that the soldier becomes emotionally dead. His own self is systematically destroyed. He no longer trusts or perhaps even believes in his own feelings, and from there on he has no self-reference point for imagining the self in others.

'My actions'

A child learns soon enough that his actions are his own. Free-will is his prerogative. He might do this, he might do that, he can say yes, he can say no. *He* chooses; and with free-will comes the right and the duty to self-determination and self-criticism. But not so for a soldier:

> Signs of respect for superiors and the Army are coercively and continuously demanded as a way of constantly reinforcing recognition of the recruit's subservient and stigmatized role… Obedience instilled in basic training leads effectively to dependence with a reliance upon and acceptance of the will of others. Responsibility for one's own welfare and for the consequences of one's acts is relinquished and remains habitually in the hands of superiors.[9]

Thus obedience absolves the soldier from self-criticism. He no longer wonders about 'his' actions, because his actions become 'theirs'.

'Affect'

The idea that other people are 'affected' – I mean affected internally – by what is done to them is the natural extension of discovering feelings in oneself. As a child grows up he learns – and this is crucial –

to *talk* about other people in those terms. Language and thinking reinforce each other. The words he has learned – pain, love, fear, etc. – become a way of probing and exploring his own and other people's minds. Indeed, the words themselves can act as a powerful spur to his own feelings, evoking as he uses them or hears them an empathic response – a shade of the same feeling in himself.

But the corollary is this: a language stripped of feeling blocks understanding, and reins in empathy. When communication and feeling are not wanted, a change of *language* is one of the most effective tricks of all:

> Even his accustomed language pattern must be renounced, and college graduates are reduced under the taunts of sarcastic drill sergeants to a vocabulary of monosyllabic conformity interspersed with obscenities adopted from their mentors.[10]

The soldier's language becomes no longer a language of affect. Enemies if they are not 'zapped' are 'liquidated'. Bombs if they are not used to 'fry' the 'dinks' are used for 'demographic targetting'. Away from the immediate battlefield, monosyllabic obscenities are quickly replaced by polysyllabic euphemisms, equally lacking in affective content and in some ways equally obscene. The 'experiment' at Hiroshima was, Truman said, 'an overwhelming success'. The Nazis had a 'final solution' for the Jewish problem. 'We sterilize the area prior to the insertion of the Revolutionary Development Team,' says the colonel, in Mary McCarthy's report from Vietnam.

Thus the language of war becomes a cover, not a probe: a way of talking about pain and death

without really talking about it. No one can have any feeling for 'sterilization', 'final solutions' and 'experiments': we are not even tempted to feel any genuine repugnance towards them, because at the level of feeling they do not mean anything at all.

'You'

'You' are, by assumption, another human being. That is why I *mind* about you, and expect you to have feelings like my own. But during the training of a soldier:

> Overriding all other issues is a strong racist flavour that pervades the attitude of the military ... An essential element in most massacres or atrocities is a preceding psychological step in which the victims are relabelled and identified as being different, inferior or even subhuman, which then allows [the soldier] to commit acts that would be unthinkable if the victims were viewed as human beings like him.[11]

Thus the victim is killed in the soldier's mind, even before he gets killed by his gun. 'Gooks', 'slopes' and 'dinks' for the GIs in Vietnam. 'Jewish vermin' for the Nazis. Huns, wogs, reds, rats, swine, hyenas, imperialist running dogs, you name it: anything but plain, warm people like ourselves. In a public speech in Denver in 1864 Colonel Chivington advocated the killing and scalping of all American Indians including children. 'Nits make lice,' he declared. A few months later this is what occurred:

> Everyone I saw dead was scalped. I saw one squaw cut open with an unborn child lying by her side. I saw the body of White Antelope with the privates

cut off, and I heard a soldier say he was going to make a tobacco pouch out of them... I saw a little girl about five years of age who had been hid in the sand; two soldiers discovered her, drew their pistols and shot her, and then pulled her out of the sand by the arm.[12]

It does not take a special sort of man to be a soldier. Stanley Milgram conducted a famous study on 'obedience to authority'. Experimental subjects, chosen at random from the general population, were told they were to take part in a learning experiment where they were to play the role of teacher, while another person (Milgram's confederate) took the part of learner. The learner was supposed to memorize a list of word-pairs, and the job of the teacher – seated in another room – was to help him learn by giving him an electric shock whenever he made an error. The more errors the learner made, the stronger the shock he was given – up to 450 volts, at which point the switch on the shock-generator was marked 'Danger! Severe Shock'. In fact no shocks were actually given; the situation was rigged. The responses the subject thought he was getting from the learner were from a tape-recording with prearranged right and wrong answers. As the errors increased and the punishment along with it, the subject heard howls of pain, demands to be let out, and finally silence from the room next door. The real purpose of the experiment was to see how far the subject would go in giving someone electric shocks, when prompted to do so by an authority, the experimenter.

How many subjects would you expect to carry on right up to the 450 volt mark? People's usual estimate is 1 per cent. In fact, some 65 per cent, almost two-thirds of the subjects, did so. Milgram wrote in 1973:

> I am forever astonished that when lecturing on the obedience experiments in colleges across the country, I faced young men who were aghast at the behaviour of experimental subjects and proclaimed that they would never behave in such a way, but who, in a matter of months, were brought into the military and performed without compunction actions that made shocking the victim seem pallid. In this respect they are no better and no worse than human beings of any other era who lend themselves to the purposes of authority and become instruments in its destructive processes.[13]

Some of us may still believe that we ourselves would never do it. Others may recognize that 'There, but for the grace of God, go we.' But what disturbs me at another level is the possibility that, even in our everyday civilized relationships, 'there' – in the grip of dehumanizing institutions – many of us already are.

Rousseau's story of the noble savage was a kind of thought-experiment – a guess about how things might once have been and what it would mean if they had been. 'The state of nature', he wrote, 'may exist no longer, may never have existed, probably never will exist,' but it is something of which 'it is necessary to have a just idea in order to judge well our present state.' The story of the 'ignoble savage' going to war is demonstrably more than a thought-experiment. Such people do exist. Here, for the record, is another one of them being interviewed, Steve, a member of the US Navy's Special Forces:

> When I got to action in Vietnam the only thing that
> was going through my mind was exactly what was
> planned, and that was to kill Communists. And I
> became a machine, a very effective machine.[14]

But for all their documentary reality, such people
have a kind of mythic quality. Steve's reality is the
reality of a character in a Greek tragedy, or a man
met on Gulliver's travels, or painted by Bosch. Like
the noble savage he might as well be an invention.
Suppose an artist *had* invented Steve, what would
he have been trying to tell us about human beings in
general? The artist idealizes, caricatures, distorts;
he shows us things which do not necessarily exist,
but which if they did would help us to make sense
of that which does. Do *we* need the idea of Steve in
order to judge well *our* present state?

I think we do, and that we could take the lesson
of the soldier several ways. I identified earlier four
weak links in the imaginative chain from 'I' to
'you': the concept of self, of responsibility for one's
own actions, of affective depth and of kinship to
other human beings are all threatened by the sys-
tematic bullying of basic training. But they are vulnerable also to the more ordinary pressures of
civilized society: pressures towards specialization,
respect for institutional authority, submission to a
'greater good'.

Let us consider, just because it seems such an
unfair case to consider, the example of a hospital
doctor. How do you transform a young man – who
could have become anything or anybody – into the
white-coated physician who talks down to both
laymen and nurses, has no time either for his
patients or himself, and does repair jobs on people
as if he were doing a repair job on a car?

You promise him a title for a start, *Dr* So-and-so. From the moment a student enters medical school he is led to believe that never again will he be quite like other people. He becomes a novice, awaiting admission to mysteries which will come only after an apprenticeship of considerable suffering. He becomes isolated from his peers, and in many schools encouraged to conform to the traditions of heartiness and philistinism which in Britain have been the tradition of medical students. The early years of his training are characterized by a requirement to amass without question a pile of anatomical and physiological knowledge (much of which has and could have no bearing on any future needs). Trial by examination passed, he continues his apprenticeship as a 'houseman' in a hospital. Hours are long, conditions awful, and his social life in ruins. At this stage signs of respect are continuously (if not actually coercively) demanded. He must speak and dress in the right way, and accept that his personal opinions should be subordinate to those of the 'consultant' to whom he is attached. Responsibility – when finally he is given responsibility – does become nominally the apprentice doctor's own. But he has neither time, nor in many cases the experience or clinical judgement to exercise responsibility effectively. He is thrown into situations where he has to take decisions about people in whom he has no personal interest, under conditions where he cannot always know what the consequences will be. The burden of responsibility if it was accepted would prove unbearable; but it is not accepted – the profession itself takes responsibility and will cover up for errors publicly while excusing them privately. The doctor is, in any case, protected from the human consequence of his decisions by a replacement language, which speaks of people as cases and of their ailments as pathological disorders.

Now, maybe this is an exaggerated picture. But it is no exaggeration to say that the elements of basic training are there, and they could be recognized equally in the training of a lawyer, a journalist, a politician, a car salesman, a policeman, a priest. Society takes an ordinary young man or woman and transforms them into Detective Sergeant A., Reverend Father B., Assistant Secretary C. – and in every case turns a person, to some degree, into a machine: separated from other people by custom and by language, wielding authority and also respecting it, self-defined cogs in the larger machin-

ery of state. Perhaps it is inevitable. But it is also planned.

When Plato set out in *The Republic* his prescription for how an ideal state might be run, he argued explicitly that the interests of the community would be served best if people were assigned as early as possible to particular exclusive roles.[15]

> We forbid our shoemaker to try his hand at farming or weaving or building and tell him to stick to his last... Similarly with other trades, we assign each man to the one for which he is naturally suited, and which he is to practise throughout his life to the exclusion of all others.

For a man even so much as to imagine he might change his job would threaten the efficient running of the state. People must be prevented, therefore, from getting the idea that one person can play a multiplicity of roles. Even actors – in so far as acting was allowed at all – must be limited to playing a single part. Hence:

> If we are visited in our state by someone who has the skill to transform himself into all sorts of characters and represent all sorts of things, and he wants to show off himself and his poems to us, we shall treat him with all the reverence due to a priest and giver of rare pleasure, but shall tell him that he and his kind have no place in our city, being forbidden by our code, and send him elsewhere, after anointing him with myrrh and crowning him.

The principle of fixity of occupation and expectation was to be imposed most severely of all in the three-layered class system, and – to help make sure of it – it would be sensible to encourage loyalty and submission to the system with the help of a 'Royal Lie':

> Now I wonder if we could contrive one of those convenient stories we were talking about a few minutes ago, some magnificent myth that would in itself carry conviction to the whole community? ... We shall address our citizens as follows: 'You are all of you in this land, brothers. But when God fashioned you, he added gold in the composition of those of you who are qualified to be Rulers (which is why their prestige is greatest); he put silver in the Soldiers; and iron and bronze in the farmers and the rest.'

'That is the story,' says Plato's mouthpiece, Socrates, 'do you think there is any way of making people believe it?' ... 'Not in the first generation, but you might succeed with the second and later generations.'

Unfortunately, however, history suggests that people will only too readily believe it. Since Plato's time *The Republic* may never have been realized at a practical level (though the German Third Reich came alarmingly close to it); but at a psychological level it is the state in which an increasing number, perhaps the majority of people live today.

I would not fall into the romantic trap of believing it was all better before social institutions came. Indeed, given everything I said in the last chapter about the ways in which civilized culture has developed techniques for communicating human experience, I cannot now argue that the whole thing is a failure. I do believe, however, that much of this potential has been undermined, and not just in the ways I hinted at before. The advance of civilization, instead of making people more secure in their knowledge of who and what they are, has fundamentally had the opposite effect. On one level the world is better managed and scientifically explained than it ever was before; and human beings are more accessible than ever. Yet, despite that, people have lost confidence in their own powers. Few any longer *feel* the power of understanding in their daily lives.

A desert bushman or a forest Indian, for all his relative unsophistication, still lives in a world which he has either made or watched being made. There is almost nothing of which he does not have a first-person understanding. His house is made with sticks which he has cut, or from mud which he himself puddles and places and sees bake in the sun. He eats food which he himself digs from the earth, or shoots down in the field. He learns nothing except what he learns from a kinsman or friend. Everything – but much more significant, every person – has a place and a history and an explanation. He *knows* the people of his community. He has seen them being made, and has explored their world for himself. He may not himself become the medicine man, the great hunter, the painter ... or the village idiot. Those that do are none the less his people and his friends, made of the same human stuff of which he is made.

But for us, *people* like the objects around us are becoming, so we believe, more and more apart from us. We are increasingly dependent on strangers with strange skills. 'Experts' ... we don't see them being made, don't know where they've come from. They have been formed in some distant factory: 'law school', 'university'. We no more

expect to understand them than we expect to understand the workings of a television, or the origins of washing powder. The doctor or the lawyer or the teacher is delivered to us like the paper or the milk. We are glad to have them, but we do not ask any questions.

'Doctors understand illness, I don't... Teachers understand education, MPs understand politics, generals understand war, etc... Leave it to them.' But more depressingly still, this sense of our own incompetence spills over into our dealings with the world at large. 'Oh, I wouldn't know about him, he's an artist... I don't understand the younger generation... Very unpredictable, these Arabs... Gay people live in a wholly different world... She's a film-star, not one of us... Of course, women are a closed book to me... I can't imagine what it would be like to vote Conservative, etc.' And behind it all the plea of 'Little me, I'm just myself; I can't take on, even in imagination, another person's role.' Charlotte Brontë wrote in a fit of self-abasement: 'I know my own sentiments, I can read my own mind, but the minds of the rest of man and woman kind are to me sealed volumes, hieroglyphical scrolls, which I cannot easily either unseal or decipher.'[16] President Carter, before meeting with Chairman Brezhnev, believed it necessary to be coached by experts about the mysteries of something called the 'Russian mind'.

Doctors, lawyers, priests, criminals, blacks, gays, feminists, Russians, Arabs... We recognize that they are people. But given our growing lack of trust in our private powers of understanding, we do not recognize that they are perhaps people *just like us*. We forget – conveniently sometimes – their naked humanness. We do not see that these strangers are,

in fact, made in our own image, and that *we* therefore have the power to make them in our own imagination.

We may call it 'respect': respect for other
people's differentness. We may even believe – as
liberals – that we are doing another race or creed or
sex an honour by crediting them with mysterious
inner qualities. Yet the assumption that we are in
fact ignorant of other people's lives and ways of
thinking is generally as insulting to them as to ourselves. To them, because we do not give them the
credit for being as human and ordinary as we ourselves are; to ourselves, because we do not recognize our own remarkable capacity for entering in
imagination into *any* human life.

Sartre wrote:

> Every one of us must choose himself, but in choos-
> ing for himself he chooses for all men. For in effect,
> of all the actions a man may take in order to create
> himself as he wills to be, there is not one which is
> not creative, at the same time, of an image of man
> such as he believes he ought to be... Our re-
> sponsibility is thus much greater than we had sup-
> posed, for it concerns mankind as a whole... In
> fashioning myself I fashion man.[17]

But our responsibility is, I believe, greater than even
Sartre implied. The burden of this book has been to
show that not only our hopes for other people but
our very perception of what they *are* is founded on
what we think about ourselves. It is not just that in
our actions each of us chooses for all mankind, it is
that in our souls each of us is the template for all
mankind. Any constraint – philosophical, political,
religious, military – which limits a man's sense of

his own possibilities puts *consciousness* itself in chains.

The irony is that human consciousness itself made the space for the inhuman institutions which now threaten it. The function of consciousness, I have argued, was to enable human beings individually to understand and relate to one another. It was on the back of that understanding that they were able to form the first human societies, based on sharing, cooperation, and sensitivity to one another's needs. Society gave them a liberating culture. But at the same time society created a machinery of state to which individuals have become increasingly subservient. Consciousness made the first human families, the first friendships, the first loves, it made Shakespeare and Dickens ... and it made Boot Camp, Madison Avenue, the Vatican Council and the KGB.

I can see at the end of it all a strange picture. For four thousand million years there was, as they say, darkness on the face of the waters. A moment ago in evolutionary history the torch of consciousness was lit, and blazed out to illuminate the world around each individual human being. But consciousness itself becomes encircled. Around it there forms a fringing reef of parasitic institutions. Within time, under the dead weight of these institutions – army, church, state – the island of consciousness begins to sink back into the sea. Until all we are left with is a barren atoll, capping the drowned rock of the human soul.

TEN
Epilogue

By 1897 Paul Gauguin's dream of the simple life on Tahiti had proved illusory. He was sick, depressed and short of money. On New Year's Eve, he climbed the hill behind his house with a box of arsenic in his pocket. Whether he took too much of the poison, or too little, no one knows. He vomited it up, and after lying out a few hours, dragged himself disconsolately home.

His attempt at suicide went wrong. But his attempt to leave behind him some great testament to his life succeeded. Before dying he painted an extraordinary picture, drawn on four metres of rough sacking. And he wrote on it – he said it was his signature – *D'où venons nous? Que sommes nous? Où allons nous?*

The big canvas so far as execution is concerned is very imperfect; it was done in a month without any preliminary study; I wanted to die and in this state of despair I painted it at one go... At the bottom on the right a baby sleeps. Communal life, the endless succession of beings... Two figures, clothed in purple expressing sadness, walk in the shadow of the tree of knowledge... A large figure, crouching, raises its arms in the air and watches,

173

astonished, those two persons who dare think upon their destiny... So I have finished a philosophical work on a theme comparable to that of the Gospel.[1]

Where have we come from? What are we? Where are we going? Gauguin asked those questions for and about himself, he asked them for and about the natives of the South Sea isles, he asked them ... well, he asked them because they are the kind of questions people inevitably ask. It is human nature to ask questions: the way we try to give meaning to existence, and impose order on an otherwise chaotic, pointless universe. Of all the questions we can ask, those three of Gauguin's are surely the most crucial. They are not really separate questions, but one big question taken in three bites. For only by understanding where we have come from can we make sense of what we are; only by understanding what we are can we make sense of where we are going.

> Time present and time past
> Are both perhaps present in time future,
> And time future contained in time past.[2]

But 'time past'? Eight million years ago there was an eruption in the South Pacific Ocean, and the island of Tahiti rose out of the sea. Not long after, twelve thousand miles away in Africa, another eruption would occur: a race of apes would spread from the woods on to the savannah, and begin to establish a specifically human way of life. The apes' brains doubled in size. Human intelligence evolved, and with it came new powers of imagination, insight and conscious self-awareness.

If I had to choose a single human trait to define

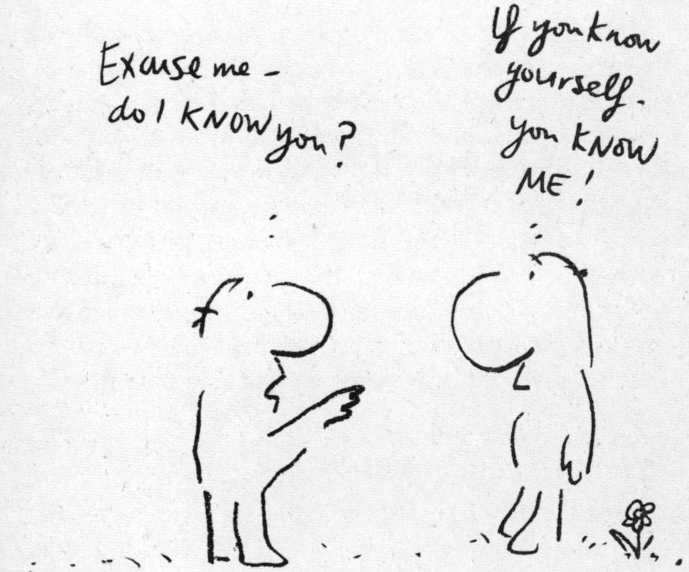
Excuse me -
do I KNOW you?
If you know
yourself.
you KNOW
ME!

what 'we are' by virtue of our evolution, it would be this: we are beings with a unique capacity to *mind* – to mind what we are and to mind what other people are. 'I can lay down for mankind a rule for our duties in human relationships,' wrote Seneca two thousand years ago, 'all that you behold is one – we are parts of one great body. Nature produced us related to one another, since she created us from the same source to the same end. She engendered in us mutual affection, and made us prone to friendships. Let this verse [by Terence] be always in your heart and on your lips: *Homo sum; humani nihil a me alienum puto* (I am a man; nothing human do I count foreign to me).'[3] But there is, as we have seen, another thing we are: we are beings who are capable of becoming foreign even to ourselves.

Insight is none the less our birthright and our greatest gift. Each of us begins life prepared by nature to create the world of other people in his own image. For a child there is no other choice. He sees in other people no more nor less than the feelings that he himself has known, and as he grows richer in himself the world around grows richer with him. The key to his future and to ours must lie in letting this childlike sense of *self*-importance live on into maturity, in the recognition that we can in the end give out only what we ourselves contain.

I am CONSCIOUS
but I don't always
LIKE IT..
I wish
I were
conscious
SILENCE

References

Chapter 1. Behind Appearances

1. Paul Gauguin, interview in the *Echo de Paris*, 23 February 1891.
2. Paul Gauguin, *Noa-Noa*, pp. 78–9, 1893, trans. J. Griffin, Cassirer, Oxford, 1961.
3. Paul Gauguin, quoted by Wayne Andersen, *Gauguin's Paradise Lost*, New York, 1971.
4. August Strindberg, quoted by Wayne Andersen, ibid.
5. Denis Diderot, 'Supplement to the Voyage of M. Bougainville', 1784, in *Diderot, Interpreter of Nature: Selected Writings*, trans. J. Stewart and J. Kemp, Lawrence and Wishart, London, 1937.
6. John Dryden, *The Conquest of Granada*, 1672.
7. Jean-Jacques Rousseau, *Discourse on Inequality*, 1755.
8. Jean-Jacques Rousseau, ibid.
9. Denis Diderot, ibid.
10. Charles Darwin, *The Autobiography of Charles Darwin*, in *Life and Letters of Charles Darwin*, ed. Francis Darwin, John Murray, London, 1887.
11. Charles Darwin, *Journal of Researches*, Murray, London, 1845.
12. Charles Darwin, ibid.
13. Charles Darwin, 'B Notebook', B25, in *Metaphysics, Materialism and the Evolution of Mind*, ed. Paul H. Barrett, University of Chicago Press, Chicago, 1980.
14. Quoted in *Life and Letters of Charles Darwin*, ed. Francis Darwin, John Murray, London, 1887.
15. Paul Dirac, 'The evolution of the physicist's picture of nature', *Scientific American*, May 1963.
16. Denis Diderot, 'On the Interpretation of Nature', 1754, in

The Irresistible Diderot, ed. J. H. Mason, Quartet, London, 1982.

Chapter 2. *Natural Psychologists*

1. Charles Darwin, 'M notebook', M84, 1838, in *Metaphysics, Materialism, and the Evolution of Mind*, ed. Paul H. Barrett, University of Chicago Press, Chicago, 1980.
2. Milan Kundera, *The Unbearable Lightness of Being*, p. 30, Faber and Faber, London, 1984.

Chapter 3. *The Ghost in the Machine*

1. René Descartes, *Discourse on Method*, 5, 1637, trans, A. Wollaston, Penguin, Harmondsworth, 1960.
2. Henry More, letter to Descartes, 1648, quoted by Bernard Williams, *Descartes*, Penguin, Harmondsworth, 1978.
3. René Descartes, letter to Plempius, 1637, quoted by Bernard Williams, ibid.
4. Nicholas Humphrey, 'Seeing and nothingness', *New Scientist*, 53, 682, 1972.
5. L. Weiskrantz et al., 'Visual capacity in the hemianopic field following a restricted occipital ablation', *Brain*, 97, 709, 1974.
6. T. H. Huxley, quoted by Lloyd Morgan, *Animal Behaviour*, Edward Arnold, London, 1900.
7. Charles Darwin, 'B Notebook', B232, 1838, in *Metaphysics, Materialism and the Evolution of Mind*, ed. Paul H. Barrett, University of Chicago Press, Chicago, 1980.
8. Charles Darwin, *Origin of Species*, John Murray, London, 1859.
9. Lloyd Morgan, *Animal Behaviour*, Edward Arnold, London, 1900.

Chapter 4. *The Inner Eye*

1. J. B. Watson, *Behaviorism*, Routledge & Kegan Paul, London, 1928.
2. B. F. Skinner, 'The steep and thorny path to a science of behaviour', in *Problems of Scientific Revolution*, ed. R. Harre, Oxford University Press, Oxford, 1975.
3. Thomas Hobbes, *Leviathan*, 1651, ed. M. Oakeshott, Oxford University Press, Oxford, 1946.
4. Ludwig Wittgenstein, *Philosophical Investigations*, Blackwell, Oxford, 1958.

Chapter 5. Is There Anybody There?

1. Anatole France, *Penguin Island*, 1908, trans. A. W. Evans, Franklin Watts, London, 1931.
2. David Premack and Guy Woodruff, 'Does the chimpanzee have a theory of mind?', *Behavioural and Brain Sciences*, 4, 515, 1978.
3. Immanuel Kant, *Critique of Judgement*, 58, 1790, trans. E. F. Carritt, Oxford University Press, Oxford, 1931.
4. A. N. Whitehead, *Science and the Modern World*, Cambridge University Press, Cambridge, 1926.
5. H. S. Jennings, *Behavior of the Lower Organisms*, Columbia University Press, New York, 1906.

Chapter 6. Sentimental Education

1. Inge Bretherton and Marjorie Beeghly, *Developmental Psychology*, 18, 906, 1982.
2. St Augustine, *Confessions*, I.vii, *c*. AD 400.
3. Friedrich Nietzsche, *Daybreak*, 1881, in *A Nietzsche Reader*, trans. R. J. Hollingdale, Penguin, Harmondsworth, 1977.
4. George Eliot, *The Mill on the Floss*, 1860, Penguin, Harmondsworth, 1979.
5. Robert Southey, letter to G. C. Bedford, 30 September 1796.
6. Lloyd deMause, 'The evolution of childhood', in *The History of Childhood*, ed. L. deMause, Souvenir Press, London, 1976.
7. Dream quoted by C. W. Kimmins, 'Children's dreams', in *A Handbook of Child Psychology*, ed. C. Murchison, Clark University Press, 1931.

Chapter 7. A Book at Bedtime?

1. Letter from J. A. Higham, *Listener*, 28 May 1981.
2. Kate Phillips, interview recorded during the filming of the television series, *The Inner Eye*, 1985.
3. David Foulkes, *Children's Dreams: Longitudinal Studies*, Wiley-Interscience, New York, 1982.
4. Gwen Raverat, *Period Piece*, Faber and Faber, London, 1952.
5. St Teresa of Avila, *The Autobiography of St. Teresa*, trans. by Dalton, 1853.
6. David Foulkes, ibid.

Chapter 8. Other People's Dreams

1. T. S. Eliot, *The Waste Land and Other Poems*, Faber and Faber, London, 1940.
2. Alfred Lord Tennyson, *Tiresias*, 1885.
3. Chuckchee shaman, 1904, quoted by Joan Halifax, *Shamanic Voices*, Penguin, Harmondsworth, 1980.
4. Tungus shaman, quoted by Joan Halifax, ibid.
5. Caribou shaman, quoted by Joan Halifax, ibid.
6. Edgar Johnson, *Charles Dickens*, Allen Lane, London, 1953.
7. Lin Shu, preface to Charlotte Yonge's *Eagle and the Dove*, quoted by Arthur Waley, *The Secret History of the Mongols*, Allen and Unwin, London, 1963.
8. Plato, *The Republic*, 395, trans. H. D. Lee, Penguin, Harmondsworth, 1955.
9. American infantryman, quoted by Robert Jay Lifton, *Home from the War*, Wildwood House, London, 1974.

Chapter 9. Where Are We Going?

1. Charles Darwin, letter to Alexander Agassiz, 1881, quoted by C. M. Yonge, 'Darwin and coral reefs', in *A Century of Darwin*, ed. S. A. Barnett, Heinemann, London, 1962.
2. A-bomb test observer, quoted by Robert Scheer, *With Enough Shovels: Reagan, Bush and Nuclear War*, Secker and Warburg, London, 1983.
3. Hiroshima survivor, interviewed by Robert Jay Lifton, *Death in Life*, Basic Books, New York, 1968.
4. Brien M. McMahon, speech before the US Senate, 1952, quoted by Marc Barasch, *The Little Black Book of Atomic War*, Dell Publishing, New York, 1983.
5. Bertrand Russell, letter to *The Nation*, London, 15 August 1914.
6. Animal Protection Act, Third Reich, quoted by A. V. Hill, *Spectator*, 18 May 1945.
7. Vietnam veteran, interview with Mike Wallace, CBS News, in *New York Times*, 25 November 1969.
8. Peter G. Bourne, 'From Boot Camp to My Lai', in *Crimes of War*, ed. Richard Falk, Gabriel Kolko and Robert Jay Lifton, Random House, New York, 1971.
9. Peter G. Bourne, ibid.

10. Peter G. Bourne, ibid.

11. Peter G. Bourne, ibid.

12. Robert Bent, description of Cheyenne massacres, quoted by Dee Brown, *Bury My Heart at Wounded Knee*, Pan Books, London, 1972.

13. Stanley Milgram, *Obedience to Authority*, Tavistock, London, 1974.

14. Steve (Vietnam veteran), quoted by Nadia Haggar, *The Listener*, 9 May 1985.

15. Plato, *The Republic*, 374, 397, 415, trans. H. D. P. Lee, Penguin, Harmondsworth, 1955.

16. Charlotte Brontë, letter to Ellen Nussey, 1833, quoted by Margaret Lane, *The Brontë Story*, Fontana, London, 1969.

17. Jean-Paul Sartre, *Existentialism and Humanism*, 1946, trans. Philip Mairet, Methuen, London, 1960.

Chapter 10. Epilogue

1. Paul Gauguin, letter to Daniel de Monfried, February 1898, quoted by Bengt Danielsson, *Gauguin in the South Seas*, Allen and Unwin, London, 1965.

2. T. S. Eliot, *Four Quartets*, 'Burnt Norton', Faber and Faber, London, 1935.

3. Seneca, *Epistolae Morales*, Letter XCV, 1st century.

Index